Sue Mayfield is the auth ... :s,
three of which (*Blue, Voi* ... :d
for the Carnegie Medal. ...)k
Award and the 2005 Heartland Award in the ... re
it was published as *Drowning Anna*. *Un an après* (the French
edition of *Damage*) won the 2011 Prix Polar de Jeunesse.
Hill of the Angels is her ninth novel and the first with a
historical setting. After living for many years in West Yorkshire, Sue Mayfield is now based in Gloucestershire, where she
works as a writer, therapist and arts-in-health facilitator. She
is currently Writer-in-Residence with Cheltenham Festivals
and Gloucestershire Hospital Education Service.

www.suemayfield.co.uk

HILL
OF THE
ANGELS

SUE MAYFIELD

First published in Great Britain in 2016

Society for Promoting Christian Knowledge
36 Causton Street
London SW1P 4ST
www.spck.org.uk

British Library Cataloguing-in-Publication Data
A catalogue record for this book is available from the British Library

ISBN 978–0–281–07641–3
eBook ISBN 978–0–281–07642–0

Typeset by Graphicraft Limited, Hong Kong
Manufacture managed by Jellyfish
First printed in Great Britain by CPI
Subsequently digitally printed in Great Britain

eBook by Graphicraft Limited, Hong Kong

Produced on paper from sustainable forests

For T,
who loves the hills,
woods and streams
of West Yorkshire

1660

Prologue

The bells – mute and still for so long – are ringing out in jubilant clangs. Ringing so loud their song resounds around the valley and seems to make the earth dance. Ringing like laughter that cannot be suppressed – on and on, as though the bells themselves might burst with joy.

On the hill above Middleholme a boy is running. His bare feet sink into the soft spring grass and as he slows to cross the wetland beneath the crags black peaty water oozes between his toes. Overhead a lapwing circles him, shrieking. Higher up the hill the boy's sister – dark hair spilling behind her like pitch – leaps from boulder to boulder, climbing up towards the Winstone Rocks. She is singing – imitating the rhythm of the bells. At the sound of her voice a rabbit darts for cover.

Further back, their mother, a sleeping baby tied to her waist with a woollen shawl, stops to catch her breath and shouts, 'I'll be there before both of you. Just watch me!' She laughs and strokes the baby's cheeks, which are squashed against her blouse like ripe fruit. Then she turns to the man with a beard the colour of autumn leaves, resting on an outcrop of rock beside her, and kisses the top of his head. They gaze together across woods and scattered farms to Middleholme, where the silver band of the river snakes along the valley bottom, and the parish church crouches with its squat black tower.

It is May. Hawthorn blossom dots the hillsides like clumps of snow and yellow irises wave like flags in the mud. In the grass, bright green shoots of bracken are uncurling like caterpillars waking to the sun. In the streets of the town, far below, they can see crowds and, in the market square, a ring of people dancing to a piper's tune. The woman smiles, feeling the afternoon warmth on her face.

At the top of the hill, the girl – outrunning her brother – reaches the rocks first, and squeezes herself through the gap in the stones. Then, from inside the cool cave she squeals, 'They're here! Come and see!'

1640

Abigail

I was ten years old when I first spoke to Grace Fowler. I'd seen her before, with her hair like ripe corn, riding behind her father on his handsome horse. I'd seen her on Sundays, too, squeezed in a pew beside her mother and her sisters – all in a row, like shiny beads on a string.

*

It was September – apple time. I'd taken the pony to the tanner's yard beside the bridge to get some leather straps for Father and was heading home again, up past the church, with its clock face like a blue moon. The vicar's house is just across from the church porch, a square stone house – quite grand – with high walls all around and an iron gate. Beside the gate is an apple tree that grows right over the wall and trails its branches in the lane. That year – 1640, the year my story begins – it was completely covered in scarlet apples – so many of them that they were spilling on to the cobbles.

As we passed by, the pony – who was always inclined to be both greedy and idle – stopped stubbornly and began to eat the fallen fruit from about his feet.

7

'What's your pony's name?' someone said. I looked up and there was Grace Fowler, sitting on the vicarage wall, higher than my head.

'He doesn't have one,' I said. For as long as I could remember we had referred to him simply as 'the pony'.

'All ponies should have names,' she said, swinging her legs and smiling at me. 'I would call him Pigeon,' she said, 'because he's the colour of a pigeon and as plump as one, too. Pi-geon?' She plucked an apple off the tree and stretched her palm towards the pony, making a clicking sound with her tongue. The pony looked up, took the apple and chomped noisily.

'He likes his name,' Grace said.

'No, he likes your apples,' I replied, and she laughed.

'I can see everything from up here,' she said suddenly. 'Why don't you come up here, too?'

It was getting late. I had been gone several hours. Mother would be needing me back at the farm. If the pony ate too many apples he'd get the colic and kick his belly all night long. I knew I'd best be on my way. But there was something about Grace Fowler – some brightness – that drew me to her, even then. So I hooked the pony's reins on to the overhanging branch and scrambled on to the wall, skinning my knees as I went.

Grace was right. From the wall's top I could see all of Middleholme. The market square with its stone cross and the hot glow of the smithy's forge and the river sloshing under the bridge beside the tanner's shop with its rows of stretched hides. I could see the stocks, too, and the baker's

8

and the apothecary's and – high on the brow of the hill – I could see the Winstone Rocks, leaning together like two stone cows. This was my world. This was everything I knew. And back then, in my eleventh year, I had no inkling of the things that were about to happen to us.

'Look,' said Grace, touching me on the shoulder. 'Thomas Sunderland's house is almost made. Soon he will come and live in it.'

Down the lane, a stone's throw from the vicarage, was a brand new house, its golden walls fresh minted, doors unhung, windows as yet unglazed. I thought of Thomas Sunderland with his three fine sons and his loping grey dogs. Thomas Sunderland was a cloth merchant, one – according to my mother – on whom the Lord had smiled. 'The sun shines on the righteous,' she said. 'God has blessed him and he has prospered.'

His house was beautiful – elegant and well-proportioned. Standing in the doorway where the oak door would shortly hang, balancing on a wooden trestle, chisel in hand, was Joseph the stonemason. He was carving something into the lintel, tip-tapping with his hammer, chipping into the surface of the stone. Alongside him, watching carefully and patiently handing him his tools, was his apprentice – a boy with red hair, not much older than Grace and me. I'd seen the boy before but I didn't know his name. Not then.

Grace called to the boy and he glanced round, blushing to see us sitting on the wall, staring. Grace spoke again, her voice clear and loud.

'What is your master carving?' she asked.

'An angel,' the boy replied.

Before I knew it, Grace had climbed down off the wall and was tugging at the hem of my skirt.

'Come with me,' she said, 'to get a closer look.'

I lowered myself down into the street and Grace seized my hand, pulling me towards Master Sunderland's house until we could clearly see the figure that was appearing above the door's frame. I could see a face – its downturned chin, the roundness of its cheek, the curve of its nose – then a shoulder . . . a wisp of hair . . . two hands clasped together – all emerging miraculously from the rock. Particles of stone were falling like sawdust, gathering in tiny piles on the ground below. I couldn't say how long we watched – I was mesmerized by the sound of the tools and by the sight of the angel, becoming more substantial with each blow of the hammer.

After a time Grace spoke again, this time in a whisper.

'How does your master know what an angel looks like?' she said. The apprentice boy shook his head. 'I dunno,' he said.

'Will it have wings?' she whispered.

'I expect so,' the boy answered.

'It *must* have wings,' Grace said. 'All angels have wings!'

Grace said this with such certainty that I asked if she had seen angel. She looked at me astonished and said, 'Only in pictures.'

'I've seen angels,' I said suddenly, startled by my own boldness.

Grace stared at me, eyes wide with curiosity.

'Where?' she said.

I hesitated a moment, uncertain whether to disclose my secret. Then I pointed, up the hill, to the Winstone Rocks that sit above our house.

'There,' I said quietly.

Without warning, Grace took both my hands in hers and kissed me.

'Show me,' she said, her face awash with delight. 'Please show me.'

Grace

The church clock is striking six when we set off up the hill. The sun is just beginning to slip in the sky, casting reddish light across the fell so that it gleams chestnut like the sides of Father's horse (whose name is Falcon).

We leave the cobbled path where the spring bubbles up just below Top Slack and cut across the moor. The ground is uneven and tussocky, full of bristly grass and clumps of heather and boggy pools. I pick my way slowly, watching where I put my feet but, despite my care, the hems of my skirt are soon splattered with mud.

Abigail is a faster walker than I am, being taller and stronger and more accustomed to climbing the hill. I watch her striding up ahead of me – her mop of tangled hair, the colour of tree bark, bobbing on her shoulders. As we get higher, a chill wind is blowing, rustling the bracken and flattening the spears of bog grass in its path. We pass a group of sheep huddled under the crags. Seeing them shelter there, I wrap my arms about myself for warmth and quicken my pace, the sooner to be out of the wind.

From the window of the room where I have slept for the past five years I can see the Winstone Rocks sitting on the brow of the hill, lumpy and grey. Sometimes I have watched them for minutes on end – perhaps hours, even. As the sun moves across them they seem to change shape, like clouds, and at nightfall their silvery surface catches the last rays so that they flash like hot coals. Today, as we approach them, they loom larger and seem more substantial – more like a fortress. I have never been so close to the rocks before, nor so high above the town. As I get nearer I can see that what looks, from a distance, like a single grey mass is actually several stones, knobbly as ham bones, stacked untidily – some of them resting one on top of another. Grass and nettles are growing around them and, in the dimples and crevices, rainwater has collected in shiny puddles.

Abigail waits for me in the shelter of the largest rock. I tuck in beside her, a little out of breath from the climb.

'They're in here,' she says, lowering her voice as though speaking too loud might cause them to flee like startled creatures, and pointing to a space formed where this rock leans against its nearest neighbour. The space between the rocks makes a long dark sliver that looks like the parting in a pair of curtains. It is quite narrow – barely wider than a hand's span at the top.

'Wait,' Abigail says, pressing her finger to her lips. She dips down and, twisting her hips and shoulders sideways like a key in a lock, she wriggles though the gap and disappears from view. I wait a moment, my heart beating fast with anticipation, and then her face appears again between the stones, red-cheeked and smiling.

'Close your eyes,' she says. As I do so she takes hold of one of my hands and draws me towards her. I shuffle my feet gingerly, groping with my other hand, fingertips brushing the rough sugary rock. When I find the space I ease my body into it.

'Duck down,' Abigail says. 'Just one more step.'

I crouch low, feeling the rock pressing against my shoulders and back. In the distance I hear a bird's shrill call.

'Now look!' Abigail says, and I open my eyes to find myself in a cave just big enough for the two of us – scooped hollow like the belly of a whale. Squinting in the semi-darkness it takes a moment for my eyes to adjust. I blink hard. Then I see them . . .

Angels, no bigger than my thumb – three of them and a fourth, fainter one, like a phantom, hovering behind – dancing on the wall of the cave. I stare in wonder at their tiny winged bodies, shimmering white.

Abigail looks at me and then back at them. Then she speaks, more loudly this time, quoting from the Psalms.

'He shall give his angels charge over thee, to keep thee in all thy ways,' she says. Instinctively, I answer 'Amen'. Then, crouching low on the cool rocky floor, we watch, in reverent silence, the delicate, flickering forms.

'Let's call this the Hill of the Angels,' I whisper.

Abigail

I saw them first on a day in July – a summer-winter day when fierce sunshine gave way to an icy barrage of hailstones, which the returning sun then melted as quickly as they had come. I was travelling with Father to the wool fair in Ripon, the pony's shoulders piled high with oily fleeces from our sheep. The packhorse route climbs steeply from Top Slack – up to the crags and then north towards the lower ground. We were only half a mile from home when the sky turned – fast as blinking – from blue to grey and hailstones big as rabbit droppings rattled from the sky, causing our hands and faces to sting as though we had been lashed with a whip. As quickly as we could – given that we were laden with baggage – we left the path and took cover beside the Winstone Rocks. That was when I discovered the cave with its gritty walls and its doorway just wide enough to let me through. I sheltered there, in this damp, mossy room, until the storm had passed and the sun blazed once more across the valley.

I'm certain they weren't there at the beginning. Not when I first entered the cave. Then, there was only greyness and gloom. Fat pellets of ice had settled in the creases in my clothing, and where hailstones had lodged in my collar and hair now big drips of water were coursing down my skin. I could hear the hail drumming against the rock under which I sheltered and Father's soft voice as he sang comfort to the pony in the lee of the stones. Then the drumming stopped.

'The clouds have blown over, lass. We can be on our way again now,' Father said, and I stood up from the rocky ledge where I was crouching.

That was when they came. The dancing angels. Leaping brightly on the wall of the cave. The company of heaven. Tapered wings and white robes. And hair streaming like bog cotton.

*

Father was always one to sing. He'd sing as he sheared the bony sheep, sing as he cut the hay, sing as he carried sacks of oats to the corn mill at Blackwater Foss. He'd sing as he dug or chopped or worked the loom, sing to the pony, sing to our scrawny chickens and sing to our ginger-bristled pig. When I was still small enough to carry on his shoulders, he'd fetch me about the fell, singing as he went. Sometimes he sang the hymns we sang in church, sometimes folk songs about weavers and spinners and sheep-stealers. Sometimes he'd sing psalms – fitting a home-made tune to words that ran as deep in him as his veins. 'The Lord is my shepherd, I shall not want' . . . 'I will lift up mine eyes unto the hills, from whence cometh my help . . .' My father loved the book of Psalms. Sometimes, as he read to us by the fire, or over

16

supper, his eyes would moisten. Once when I asked him why this was, he stared into the fire grate and said, 'Inexpressible joy, Abigail. Inexpressible joy.'

*

Our home was full of joy then and the hardships we had known were as nothing compared with what was to come. I was born at Top Slack, in the curtained bed where my parents slept. I was the youngest of three children – although, in truth, I was the youngest of seven. After my eldest brother William there was a girl, stillborn. Then there was my brother Oliver, four years my senior. Between Oliver's birth and my own, my mother miscarried twice. Three years after I came into the world, there was another brother – who took my father's name of Silas. Silas took ill with a fever and died before he could walk. His tiny body is buried in the churchyard, beside the north wall.

Our family was not rich, but nor was it poor. My parents worked hard because the land was hilly and wet and the sheep tough and wiry – their fleeces too coarse to weave good cloth from the wool. For three generations the Booths had been weaver farmers and our lives were ordered by the rhythms of harvests and markets. Every Friday we would buy wool – better wool from Norfolk and the Low Countries – from the wool drivers that congregated in the market square and load it on to the pony's back. My mother would card it and spin it into yarn and then Father would weave a long strip of cloth – a kersey we called it – on the loom in the front room of our house. We'd take the piece of cloth to

Clegg's fulling mill at Coldwater Dene to be paddled and fulled with soapy earth until all the threads fused together as one piece. Then it was washed, and when it was good and soft they'd hang it on the tenter frames in the field to stretch and shrink. Come Friday, William would bundle up the kersey and take it into Middleholme to sell. There was plenty of work for all five of us what with the weaving and spinning and carding and animals to care for, and fields to dig, and all the cooking and laundry and mending. Work was what I knew. By the time I was eight years old I could spin yarn faster than my mother.

'It's your nimble fingers,' she said as I pedalled the wheel with my foot. My fingers were raw and cracked. Sometimes, in winter, they would bleed.

Grace Fowler had hands as smooth and white as goose fat. They were like angel's hands – slender and soft – and I envied them, even though I knew envy was a sin and vanity ungodly. 'Inner beauty is what counts,' my mother would say. She had no patience with ribbons and frills and fancy clothes and her own face, though kind, was plain and weathered and rough, her teeth chipped and crooked.

'Man looketh on the outward appearance,' Father read from his Bible, 'but the Lord looketh on the heart.'

I wondered what my heart looked like. What God saw when he looked at me.

*

With the hailstorm passed, Father and I continued up the causey path towards Blackmoor Top. The pony's hooves slipped and slithered on the icy slush the hailstones had left behind. As we walked, Father quoted from the Scriptures, from the twenty-fourth psalm. This was the verse he uttered every time he walked this route, the first verse he had taught me to read for myself, the verse he had urged me to memorize and to ponder upon, as though it were food – bread that I might chew and savour.

'Who shall ascend into the hill of the Lord? Or who shall stand in his holy place? He that hath clean hands, and a pure heart.' I thought of the angels in the rocky cave at the top of the hill behind Top Slack. Surely this was the hill of the Lord. Surely the cave was a holy place. And God had blessed me with a vision of the heavenly host. Because my hands were clean and my heart was pure.

Grace

CRASH! There is a loud slam followed by the hollow clump of boots on stone flags. I come to from my daydreaming with a start and catch the eye of my father who, momentarily, loses the thread of what he is saying and looks perplexed. Behind me there is shouting and the scuffle of more boots. I glance round to see who it is that is causing the disturbance and my mother, seated beside me, hisses, 'Don't stare!'

Father is in the pulpit, towering high above us, his face lit by the sun's rays that stream in rainbows through the stained glass. I love the glass, with its shining pictures and jewelled colours. I love the way it spills droplets of light on to the floor like a tapestry. Father says the glass is very ancient. He says it shouts aloud the glory of God. The window behind Father's head has more colours than a summer garden. It has blue as blue as the bluest sky and green, green hills and Jesus in a red robe − bright as haw-thorn berries. On his shoulders he carries a lamb, whiter than any I have seen on the hills around Middleholme, and around his head is a halo of shimmering gold. Father's cope is gold, too − it catches the light and glistens as he speaks.

20

He is speaking of King David, who – in Bible times – was anointed by God to rule over the people and who, Father says, was *like an angel of God*. It is his mention of an angel that has sent me skipping off into a daydream. I am thinking of our hill and Abigail's eager face and the plan I have made to take a present for the angels. Something beautiful that they will love. Something shiny and precious. I look around for Abigail Booth but Mother scowls at me so I face forward. In the pew beside me my sister fidgets and fiddles with her hair but Mother does not scowl at her because she is smaller than I am and does not have to *set an example* as I do.

The kerfuffle is continuing – getting louder and harder to ignore. Someone – a shouting man – is making his way down the aisle towards the pulpit where Father stands. I see the verger grab his arm to restrain him but the man swings his fist and lands a punch that causes the verger to cry out in pain. Father's stream of words dries to a trickle and I see, for the first time in my life, a flicker of alarm pass across his face.

I can see now who it is that is shouting. It is Isaac Clegg, whose face, broad as a shovel, is beetroot with rage. Isaac Clegg owns the fulling mill at Coldwater Dene and I know – for Father has told me – that he is a Puritan. Father says Puritans stamp on the holy mysteries with their muddied boots. He says they have no sense of splendour or occasion. Reverend Jagger, the vicar before Father, was a Puritan. He wore black like a crow and liked things simple and unadorned as porridge. Some of the folks of Middleholme want him back, though he's been gone five years. Some of the people dislike my father, though I know him to be the best and kindest man on earth. Our maid, Tabitha – who is the worst of gossips – says they dislike Father's golden cope and his crucifix and all his 'fancy newfangled stuff'. She says they hate the carved wooden rail that we kneel at for the bread and wine – that they say it's like a fence to keep cattle from roaming – and that they hate the altar with its bright flickering candles – and say that they'd rather have the table with its common linen cloth, that Reverend Jagger used before Father's time.

Father continues to speak, despite the approach of the shouting man. He is talking about the King – not King David from Bible times but King Charles, our King. He says that the King, like David, is anointed by God and rules by God's divine will. Isaac Clegg is at the foot of the pulpit steps now. He is haranguing Father with a purple mouth that spits like a kettle.

'The King is a Papist!' he says. 'The King is an enemy of the gospel.' I do not know what the word 'Papist' means but I'm sure, from the way Mr Clegg splutters it out, that it must be a bad word. Father likes the King and says he is a devout man – prayerful and sober. Not like the last king with his unseemly court. Mother says King Charles has a French wife whom some men – those of an ignorant and unrefined disposition – loathe and fear.

Father is addressing Isaac Clegg, quietly but with a steely tone which sends a shiver through me – as though a draught had blown across my back.

'The King is no enemy and you are a fool!' he says.

Isaac Clegg retaliates, speaking most rudely.

'You are the fool, Reverend Fowler, with your frills and flounces and idolatrous practices ...' I feel Mother flinch beside me and see her twist her gloves in her hands as though she were wringing out a rag. Isaac Clegg bends down and picks up a prayer book (one of our new ones – the ones Archbishop Laud introduced which Father says 'restore the dignity'). He slaps it with the palm of his hand and then he begins ranting once more, '...and this, your vile, despicable prayer book with all its mumbo-jumbo!'

Father speaks again. 'I feel I must ask you to leave, Mr Clegg,' he says. 'This disruption is an offence and an abomination.'

Isaac Clegg turns his back on the pulpit and takes three paces towards the door.

Then he turns round again and, raising his arm, he hurls the prayer book directly at Father.

'Papist!' he yells as the book strikes Father a blow on the cheek. Whereupon Mr Clegg, puffing with a sense of his own importance, opens the south door and slams it behind him.

Abigail

When I was younger I liked to walk between my brothers, each hand holding one of theirs. They'd grip me tight, lift me off my feet and swing me back and forth like the church bell and I would whoop with delight. William and Oliver were like the two stone pillars that held our gate at Top Slack. As children, they looked alike, with Mother's pale blue eyes and nut-brown hair and Father's sharp chiselled chin. Though four years the younger, Oliver grew tall and strong, so he and William seemed as twins. But while they were alike in their outward appearance my brothers were as different as night and day. William was serious, earnest, hot-tempered and easily slighted. Oliver, by contrast, was gentle, carefree and full of mischief – making us laugh with his clowning, and tumbling and wild dancing. Sometimes he would tease and bait William, prodding him into a rage, and always they would disagree. If William said he liked winter best, Oliver would prefer summer. If Oliver chose the moon, William would choose the sun. If William loved pottage, Oliver loved pudding. Oliver was Mother's favourite but I loved them both equally, as two halves of one apple. We were woven together like the cloth on the loom. I could never have imagined then that our family would rip and tear, coming apart in tatters.

*

The day Isaac Clegg threw the prayer book at Reverend Fowler – that was the day I had the first hint of the dark splits that were to come between us, for we were – all five of us, side by side in the pew – divided in our response. Mother gasped in horror at the affront, while beside her Oliver smirked with amusement. Father's face was grave and stern. For myself, I might have wrestled Isaac Clegg to the floor and punched his nose for such rudeness to my friend's father. But William – to everyone's surprise – let out a sudden cheer, such as one might make when a boy, spurred on in a contest, leaps a pole as high as his chest. It was a noise of wonderment and approval.

Walking home from church that day – grey rain falling so heavily on us that by the time we reached Top Slack our clothing was soaked through – Father spoke crossly to William. 'Isaac Clegg's behaviour was unfitting in the House of God,' he said, 'better suited to the tavern.' But William, always one to pick up wild ideas when he took the cloth to market – falling into debate with the dyers and weavers from Lumley Bridge – and full of the certainty of youth, spoke passionately in reply.

'It's about time someone spoke out. These changes have gone too far! Why should I kneel at some ungodly man-made rail to eat the Last Supper, bowing my knee like a servant when I am as much a child of God as any priest? And why should they keep us penned like animals – shut out and separate – while the parson parades about in his ribbons and finery, thinking himself more holy than the rest of us?'

I was astonished at Will's vehemence. I thought of Grace's father with his hair tied back in a velvet bow. Did he despise folk like us, as William suggested? I did not think so ...

'You're sounding like a Puritan, Will,' Oliver said, kicking a stone with the toe of his boot.

'Well, perhaps I *am* a Puritan,' Will retorted. 'Better a Puritan than a sinner.'

'We are all sinners, William,' said Father mildly. 'All saved by the blood of Christ alone, not by any merits or actions of our own.' I was holding on to Father's jerkin, sheltering from the rain in the crook of his arm. William drew alongside us, his face flashing with anger.

'Reverend Fowler would have us believe we are saved by bowing and scraping and lighting candles and sipping wine – as though his lily-white hands had worked some magic there at his *altar*.' He said the word 'altar' as though it were a filthy word – a word full of dung and maggots. 'Table', Reverend Jagger had called it. I thought of Reverend Fowler's slender white hands and of Grace's hands, too.

We had reached the door of our house by then. As we entered the passageway that separates the hearth room from the loom shed William took off his coat and shook the rain from it in drops like beads of glass.

'There've been riots in Scotland over the changes Archbishop Laud would force upon us,' he said, stamping his boots on the flags. 'The Scots will have none of it! None of his bishops. None of his popish prayer book.'

'Aye, and there's talk, too, that the King will go to war against the Scots and force them to do his bidding,' said Father, removing his hat.

'The King is a simpleton if he thinks he can force the people of this land to do what he likes. Mr Pym will teach him a lesson.' I wanted to ask who Mr Pym was but the air was now charged − full of crackle and gloom the way it is before a thunderstorm. Father and William were glaring at each other.

'Show some respect, William,' said Father, throwing a log on the fire. He bent down to poke the glowing embers and they flamed into life.

Mother was clattering plates beside the dresser.

'"Render unto Caesar that which is Caesar's", the Lord says,' she said. I knew that she meant we should honour the King and give him our loyalty and obedience, though I had no idea, nor have I still, who or what Caesar might be. William left the room, muttering something about a piece of cloth, though what he intended to do with it I do not know for it was the Sabbath when no work is done and when the loom stands silent and all our tools − our bobbins and teasels and cropping shears − lie still on the workbench and rest.

*

Mother served a cold pie made from a rabbit Oliver had trapped on the moor and we ate together around the oak

27

table. But as we ate, William continued his ranting. He spoke of Parliament and Mr Pym and pamphlets and ship money. Father had explained to me about ship money some months ago, as we led the pony home from market, his back stacked high with bundles of wool.

'The King needs it,' Father explained, 'to pay for the navy and to fight the pirates that threaten our trade.' He told me that some of the cloth we wove on our loom at Top Slack was put on ships and taken far, far away across the ocean. I liked to think of this – of our kersey with its colours of peat and bracken and heather – sailing away to lands I'd never seen. I'd never seen the ocean either, but Father had told me that it was vast and bluer than the mill pond at Blackwater Clough.

'Joseph Crabtree says some of the weavers in Lumley Bridge are refusing to pay the ship money,' Will said, wiping meat juices from his mouth with his sleeve. 'They say the tax is illegal because the King levied it without the approval of Parliament. They have written a pamphlet against it.' William pulled a crumpled sheet of paper from his pocket and waved it in front of Father. Oliver, sitting on his left side, snatched it and read it aloud with a tone of mockery.

'"What care we – spinners, weavers and sheep farmers of Lumley Bridge – for thieves, pirates and robbers of the sea! Let the coastal counties pay the ship monies! We are for land and wool!"' Will snatched it back.

'The King will tax us till we bleed,' he said. 'Are we not poor enough with just one measly rabbit to feed us all.'

'You watch, William Booth, with your pamphlets and dangerous talk,' my mother said, clattering a spoon against the dish to scrape the last of the pie on to William's plate. 'Anyway, you'll not starve,' she said, 'not while there's rabbits on the hill!'

Oliver looked disgruntled at his lack of a second helping. When he spoke his tone was spiteful.

'I heard from John Sunderland that three Puritans who'd written pamphlets against the King were made a spectacle of in London. They led them out in front of the crowd and cut off their ears. Then they branded their cheeks with searing irons.'

'That's enough, Oliver,' said Father, mopping his plate with bread.

*

Once when I was younger Father had me hold the cow by the halter while he branded her on her hindquarters. She was just a heifer then, with black fur and eyes like deep brown pools. I held fast to the rope that looped about her head, behind her ears, and stroked the rough hair under her chin. Father heated the branding iron till it throbbed orange. Then, without warning, he pressed it against her flesh where it sizzled and smoked. I felt the cow flinch with pain and saw her eyes roll back in their sockets. There was a smell of scorched fur and of burning meat and afterwards – months later when the skin had healed – I traced my fingers along the shiny lines that cut like strange pathways through the cow's fur.

Now, sat at table with my family, I thought of the three men with their burnt faces and their bleeding ears and my eyes pricked with tears.

Oliver pushed his chair back from the table, stretching his long limbs.

'Henry Sowerby says there's work to be had at Saltley Hall, with the horses,' he said. 'He says Sir James lost a stable boy to the fever.'

'We need you here, Oliver,' Mother said. 'For the weaving and the sheep. Father couldn't manage without you . . .'

'There's barely enough food or money for the five of us now – what with the price of cloth falling and falling . . .' said Oliver.

'And still we pay our ship taxes!' William shouted.

'Silence, William,' Mother said, crossly. She looked at Oliver, who was unlacing his boots. 'Would they feed you there? At Sir James's place?'

'Aye,' said Oliver, 'I'd be fed with the servants. And they'd house me, too – in a loft above the barn, if I wanted it.'

'We'd miss you here,' Father said. 'But Abigail works hard and she's getting bigger and stronger all the time.' He smiled at me across the table. I smiled back but when I thought of all the digging and scything and lifting Oliver was wont to do my heart sank.

'So my little brother will be Sir James's lapdog!' said William with a sneer.

'Not lapdog, Willy,' Oliver answered. 'Stable hand.'

I looked out of the window and saw the rain had stopped and sun was streaming down the fell. Father stood up from his chair and took his Bible from the shelf by the door. He opened it at the Psalms and, clearing his throat, he read, 'Behold, how good and how pleasant it is for brothers to dwell together in unity.' Then he closed it pointedly and left the room.

*

It was late in the afternoon when I had finished my chores – when the pots were scoured and the table wiped and the flags swept clean, for though the sheep rest on a Sunday and the spinning wheel stands idle in the workshop it seems that women must work – and girls, too. I wiped my hands on my skirt. In my pocket was half a blackbird's egg, empty and broken. I'd picked it up off the cobbles outside the barn. Grace would like it. And so would they.

*

There are two ways up to the rocks, one more strenuous than the other. I chose the easier route – it being the Sabbath – and as I climbed, the sunshine lifted my spirits. The hill, washed clean with the morning's rain, had a polished brightness about it. I tried to forget about Will's anger and the thought that Oliver might go and live at Saltley Hall and the horrifying spectacle of the branded men with no ears. Crossing sideways over the fell – our farm getting smaller and smaller – I startled a partridge that flapped and squawked in front of me.

*

I knew Grace would be there. Sometimes I can just tell. She was inside the rocks in the cool darkness of the cave, sitting on a heap of fresh-cut bracken, her knees pulled up tightly to her chest. She was singing. I heard her as I scrambled up the last few paces to the top.

31

She didn't look at me as I slipped through the space in the rocks.

'They're here . . .' she whispered. I followed her eyes across the dusky air and saw, on the cave wall, the bright shapes – three of them, and a fourth, much paler, following behind.

'What did you bring?' Grace asked. I pulled the speckled eggshell out of the folds of my skirt and placed it in her hand. It sat there on her white palm, as pale and as fragile as her. 'It's beautiful,' she said. She laid it on the ground – tenderly, reverently.

Then she made me close my eyes and hold out my own hands, just as I had made her do the first day I brought her here. Grace put something small and cold on my palm. I felt its smooth hardness with my fingertips.

'Look,' she said, and I opened my eyes. In my hand was a button, pearly and white, glistening like a shell.

'I found it in a crack in the churchyard path,' she said, smiling. 'It's treasure!'

I put it gently on the moist earth beside my blackbird's egg, at the base of the rock, where the angels could hover over it, blessing it and blessing us for our gifts. We were silent for a moment, the air heavy with wishing and with hopefulness. Then Grace laughed suddenly and hugged me tight and I smelt her hair – sweet as roses.

Grace

BANG! A sound like splitting logs, but a dozen times louder, rings out across the wood. Startled by the suddenness and loudness of the noise, the bay mare on which I am riding at a gentle trot breaks into a gallop and hurtles through the trees towards Saltley Hall. I am not an experienced horsewoman and have ridden this pony – which belongs to Lady Hallam – only twice before. Indeed, I have rarely travelled this fast on *any* horse and I find that no amount of pulling on the reins as I have been taught will make the pony slow her pace. The jolt and bump of her movements as she crashes along cause me to slip and slide and, despite my best efforts to grip the saddle, I find myself barely able to stay upright. Behind me I can hear the thunder of hooves as Lady Hallam pursues me on her own horse, but this sense of a chase only seems to make my pony travel faster.

I lean forward, grasping thick handfuls of the pony's wiry mane and lowering my head to avoid overhanging branches. The mare's neck is soapy now with sweat and the leather reins, by which I attempt to steer her, are slippery between my fingers. Suddenly we reach a fork in the track. Foolishly,

I expect the pony to take the left path, which leads out of the wood and into open parkland in front of Saltley Hall, but instead she darts to the right, jumping a low wall on to a strip of plough. I hear Lady Hallam behind me shouting, 'Hold on, Grace!' but even as she speaks I feel myself slide.

I have let go of the reins now and the pony – stretching her neck out and sensing freedom – seems to quicken her pace yet further. I am beginning to slip down her left shoulder, despite my efforts to heave myself back into the saddle.

As the mare pounds across the ploughed earth I feel her stumble slightly, hooves sinking into the heavy soil. She slows a little and I grip her foamy neck as tightly as I can, hoping she may soon tire and come to a halt. But no sooner have I tightened my grip than a second *bang!* causes the mare to buck, kicking her hind legs in the air like a rabbit, so that I am flung sideways and – losing my grip completely – fall to the ground.

Thankfully I land clear of her hooves and suffer no injury other than my wounded dignity, which Lady Hallam does much to restore, dismounting from her horse and helping me to my feet. My dress is muddied and my bonnet a little bent but I am unharmed.

'My poor child!' Lady Hallam says, stooping to wipe a smudge of dirt from my cheek. 'I had no idea Hazel would bolt at the sound of the shots. She is normally so even-tempered. Oh, look at you, my poor dear! How frightened you must have been.'

'Please, your ladyship, I am quite unhurt,' I say as she fusses over me. I smile to reassure her and bow my head, as Father has taught me to do, to show my respect.

Lady Hallam and her husband Sir James Hallam are Father's patrons. They live at Saltley Hall, a grand house that nestles in the valley half a mile outside the town. Lady Hallam has been very kind to us since Father became Vicar of Middleholme. When my mother was sick, after the birth of my sister Martha, Lady Hallam visited us in person and sent food from her own kitchen. She is gracious and gentle and a very fine horsewoman. I have been invited to ride with her at Saltley this past month, which Father says is a great honour. Tabitha, our maid, says her ladyship is barren – which means she has no children nor can ever have any – and that this means she is cursed by God but I do not think that God would curse someone so generous. The pony she gives me to ride – of whom there is now no sign at all – is called Hazel. Tabitha says Lady Hallam shows kindness to me because she has no daughter of her own and that Hazel was bought as a gift for the child she never had and now stands idle in a field, being too small and too common for her ladyship to ride upon. Mother says Tabitha says too much and her tongue will be the undoing of her but I am sad to think that Lady Hallam might be lonely for I like her very much. She has a beautiful face and a coil of fair hair that loops out from under her hat and reminds me of a skein of sheep's wool that I once found snagged on a gorse bush.

We leave the field by a gate and walk towards the house across the sloping grassland, Lady Hallam leading her sleek black horse behind her. I urge her to leave me and ride ahead to the stables but she insists on keeping me company. I feel somewhat foolish now for my lack of skill and my failure not only to make the pony stop, but also to keep hold of the reins on falling, to prevent her escape.

'I should not be surprised if she has gone straight back to her stall,' Lady Hallam says. 'Though I fear she won't much like the presence of soldiers in the stable yard.'

I am puzzled by her words. Father says a lively mind asks questions so – young as I am – I have always sought to understand the world by questioning what is and what is not. Now, as we walk together, I find my curiosity quite outstrips my manners and I cannot keep myself from asking Lady Hallam about the arrival of soldiers at Saltley Hall. She is frank in her replies.

'Sir James is mustering a regiment,' she says. 'The shots we heard were his soldiers practising their musket fire.'

I have heard my parents speaking about the King and about how he is rallying troops to fight the Scots because they fail to practise proper religion.

'Will Sir James fight the Scots?' I ask.

'Perhaps,' she says. 'And Parliament, too. Mr Pym has had Archbishop Laud imprisoned in the Tower.' Father says that Mr Pym is a traitor, who would have Parliament rule the King and not the King rule Parliament as God has decreed.

'Sir James's men will defend the King,' says Lady Hallam, 'though heaven knows most of the soldiers are just boys and farmers who can no more fire a musket than you or

I can. They must be taught. And quickly, too. So, in the coming days, I fear there will be many more bangs to frighten the horses!'

*

As we cross the drive in front of Saltley Hall a peacock struts by us, trailing his beautiful tail in the gravel. I have seen the peacocks before and marvelled at their colours. I love the oily blue that flashes like silk and the delicate combs they wear on their heads. I have seen one of them fan his tail out in a glorious shimmering ring like a halo.

Just as I am admiring the peacock, a long-legged stable boy emerges from the gateway leading Hazel by her reins. He comes towards us, the pony – her brown fur streaked with sweat – panting and walking with her head low.

'You see,' says Lady Hallam, 'she has returned safely as I said she would.' As we draw level, her ladyship reaches out her hand and strokes the pony's nose.

'Thank you, Oliver,' she says. 'Let Miss Fowler remount and lead her in a circle.' I begin to say that I would perhaps rather walk but she silences me with a look that tells me I must do as she says.

'Always remount after a fall,' she says, as the stable boy helps her on to her own horse. The boy, whose face is oddly familiar, takes hold of my leg and hoists me into the saddle. As I turn to thank him I notice he has a handsome face, which bears a smirk of amusement, and I blush again at my foolishness. The stable boy holds the pony's bridle and leads her in a circle as instructed. Seated once again on her back,

I pat the pony's neck and murmur reassuring words, though this, I suspect, is more to hide my embarrassment than to comfort the mare.

*

It is only later that I realize where I have seen the handsome smirking stable boy before. I am walking from the stable yard, crunching over the gravel drive, when it comes to me that he is Abigail's brother – Oliver Booth! At that moment I notice a peacock feather lying on the ground. I bend to pick it up, running my hand down its softness and seeing its metallic sheen catch the light and flash with rainbows.

Abigail

There is a blind beggar that sits in Middleholme churchyard beside the north porch, collecting coins in a tin bowl. His name is Old Tristram and his eyes are like dried-up seed pods. Some people say he knows the future – that he sees the way things will be more clearly than those of us with eyes.

Old Tristram was there that Friday in October when we passed the church on the way to market. His bowl was empty. When he heard the sound of the pony's hooves approaching he began to cry out.

'Woe to us, woe to us all! Blood will flow like a river. Only the merciful shall be saved.' Father paused and dropped a small coin into Old Tristram's bowl and I heard it rattle and spin.

'God have mercy on us all,' Father said quietly.

*

In the town that day, the streets were busier than usual. As well as the wool drivers with their booths and stalls, the cloth merchants with their bales of kerseys, the pens of sheep and pigs, the carts loaded with sacks of grain and flour, the quack with his table of potions and the wise woman with her bundles of herbs, there was also a large crowd gathered at the foot of the stone cross that stands in the middle of the market square. Many people were shouting and waving pieces of paper in the air like flags. As we got nearer I could see that Isaac Clegg had drawn his cart up close to the foot of the steps that surround the cross and was standing in the back of the cart addressing the crowd.

'Friends! You've heard what happened in Ireland,' he shouted, 'when the Catholic hordes defiled Protestant women, murdered Protestant children, butchered Protestant babies ...'

'Monsters, all of them!' yelled a man in the crowd.

'We've seen the pictures,' shouted another, holding a torn page above his head.

I remembered the pamphlet Will had brought home with its hideous drawings of babies spiked on pitchforks and women ripped apart like slaughtered pigs. Mother had put it in the fire saying she would not have such vileness in the house.

'We'll see worse than that before the King has finished with us!' Will had said, slamming a dead rabbit on the table. William said the rebellion in Ireland was the King's doing – that Charles had coupled himself to all Catholics by marrying a Catholic queen. Oliver, whom I'd noticed growing more favourable to the King since working at Saltley Hall, said what Will said was treason and that King Charles was as appalled by the atrocities as was every man in England.

Isaac Clegg was shouting from his cart.

'And thousands of innocent ... at Portadown ... herded into the freezing waters of the river ... naked ... hacked down by the sword if they tried to escape ... drowned ... like rats in a well ...'

'Come, Abigail,' said Father, tugging at the pony's reins to walk on, 'this is no place for children, and there's work to be done.' He took me by the arm and led me towards the cloth merchants' stalls. But no sooner had we begun to unbuckle our bale of kersey from the pony's back than a woman's scream rang out across the square. I turned and saw Isaac Clegg leaping from his cart on to the stone steps, a spade lifted high above his head.

'We must stand against these Popish devils!' he roared and with a lunge of his spade and a mighty clatter he knocked the top clean off the old stone cross.

We were, by then, too far behind the crowd to see where the chunks of flying masonry fell, but I saw a woman run by me cradling a child whose head was streaming blood. A terrible commotion ensued, with some people fleeing in terror from the square and others snatching up tools and implements with which to smash things. I heard the smithy shout, 'The Irish will come and murder us all in our beds!' and Anne Sowerby, the dyer's wife, wrung her purple hands and shrieked, 'They will slit our bellies and wash their hands in our blood!'

Then a fight broke out, with fists flying and boots flailing. Merchants' tables were overturned and I saw strips of cloth and loaves of bread strewn across the cobbles and barley grains spilling from their sacks.

41

Father quickly abandoned all hopes of selling cloth or buying wool and hurried the pony and myself over the bridge across the river.

'Will the Irish come, as they say?' I asked as we made our way quickly past Thomas Sunderland's house and up the hill.

'No, child,' he said, taking my hand. 'Do not worry yourself. It is all hot air and scaremongering!'

*

But just two days after that — on the Sunday, as we listened to the Reverend Fowler's prayers — John Sugden, a dyer from Lumley Bridge, burst into the church shouting.

'The Irish rebels are coming! We are all as good as dead! They have reached Rochdale and will be here by nightfall!' At this news some ran from the church screaming, some fell to their knees weeping and all began to talk and shout so that the Reverend Fowler, saying his prayers at the altar, was rendered as good as dumb. Climbing the steps to the pulpit he banged his fist in an attempt to restore order but terror had gripped the congregation, terror so great that he could do nothing but dismiss us with his blessing. Those that had not already left now streamed from the church, desperate to take shelter in their homes and to prepare themselves for the horrors that would surely come.

As we jostled through the north door, my mother clutching at her shawl and muttering prayers under her breath, I heard Old Tristram rattling his tin bowl. 'Rivers of blood will flow!' he cried. 'Repent and pray for mercy! Only the merciful shall be saved!'

'No,' said William, as we passed by. 'Only those that take up the sword and defend themselves shall be saved!'

*

Once we were safely inside Top Slack, Father pushed a heavy oak chest up against the door and then seated himself at the table. Opening his Bible he began to read aloud from the twenty-third psalm.

'Yea, though I walk through the valley of the shadow of death, I will fear no evil ... for thou art with me ...'

'What?' said Will, indignantly. 'Are we just going to sit here and hide like cowards? Aren't we going to fight like true Protestants?'

For once Oliver was silent. Not required at Saltley Hall on Sundays, the younger of my two brothers still joined us for the Sabbath. Watching his face in the fire's gleam I noticed it had lost its boyish sheen and that the first trace of a beard was appearing. Oliver lifted the cat on to his lap and stroked its fur rhythmically. The throaty throb of its purring filled the room. Father continued reading from the Scriptures.

'Thou preparest a table before me in the presence of mine enemies ...'

'So are we just to lie down ... like lambs at the slaughter?' Will was pacing the room, like an angry bull. 'Are we to wait helplessly as though it were doomsday?'

'Be quiet, William,' Mother said. 'You've spoken enough.'

'Surely goodness and mercy shall follow me all the days of my life ...'

Father's voice continued soft and gentle, like the cat's purr. It was like a warm, safe thing that I could creep inside. I sat in the window, my knees hugged tightly to my chest, and rocked myself as I looked west towards the Winstone Rocks. As I rocked I prayed to my angels that they would save us — save us all.

I knew later that day, with all certainty, that the angels had heard me. As the church clock struck five William, unable to contain his restlessness any longer, rode out on the pony towards Lumley Bridge (despite Mother's begging him to stay) and brought back word an hour later.

'It seems,' he said, pulling off his boots, 'that the Irish they were talking about were none other than a half-dozen Protestant families fleeing for their lives to England. They've been given shelter in Ripponden and there's no threat from them to man nor beast!' I could not tell whether William was disappointed or glad, so angry had he become of late, so spoiling for a fight. But *I* was glad and so was my mother.

'Thanks be to God,' she said. 'Thanks be to God.' Then she embraced us all, each in turn — Father and William and Oliver and me.

'The Lord is my shepherd; I shall not want,' said Father, closing his Bible with a shrug.

Grace

Three days after the rumours of the Irish I sit in the window that faces west, doing my needlework. It is afternoon – a bright October day – and violent sunlight streams in the window. I am sewing a stole that Father will wear around his neck when he celebrates the Feast of the Birth of our Lord Jesus. It is made from creamy white silk which I am embroidering with golden thread – white and gold, angels' colours. I am stitching leaves that criss-cross and entwine themselves about one another, glinting in the light. Outside, in the garden, flaming copper leaves fall from the beech tree by the gate.

The house is quiet. Mother, who is expecting another child now, is sleeping and my younger sister Martha sleeps, too. Father is writing a sermon, locked silently in his room. And Margaret – cross, fidgety Margaret – is sewing beside me, practising her stitches on a scrap of white silk. She is all elbows and thumbs and disappointed sighs.

'I cannot make it stay flat,' she says. 'Look at the way it puckers and wrinkles!'

'You must work the needle more gently,' I say. 'See! How you tug at it!'

'But it is all tangled,' she wails. She pokes at it fiercely and then yelps with pain as she pricks herself on the needle. A tiny bead of blood appears on her fingertip and spills on to the silk.

'Now look,' I say, impatiently. 'It is ruined. Take it to Tabitha.'

Margaret gets up from the window seat and flounces from the room clutching the stained cloth in her hot hands. I hear her feet clatter on the stairs as she goes in search of our maid.

Glancing from the window I notice a wisp of smoke rising from beyond the wall but think nothing of it, assuming it to be some tradesman's brazier in the lane. I continue with my work but when I look up again a few moments later, the smoke has thickened into a dense funnel of grey. It seems to be coming from the churchyard, on the north side. I can hear voices and laughter in the street. Then a cheer goes up and the sound of numerous feet stamping on cobbles as if in a clog dance.

At that moment Tabitha shrieks from an upstairs room.

'Master! Mistress! Come quickly!'

I throw my silk down on the seat and run from the room, just as Tabitha shouts again, twice as loudly. Father dashes past me in the passageway and I follow him, at great speed, upstairs into the room where I and my sisters sleep. Tabitha is standing by the window, with Martha in her arms.

'Is it the child?' my father says quickly. 'Is she unwell?'

'What is it?' asks my mother, appearing in the doorway, her hair all unpinned. 'Why are you shouting?'

'Look, my lady,' Tabitha says. 'They are burning all the holy stuff!' She points outside.

I dash to the window and stare out into the street. Beyond our wall, across the lane, on the stone flags outside the north porch where Old Tristram sits to beg, a stack of wood is burning. Great red flames leap from it towards the sky. Around it, in a ring, their faces lit up like demons, are more than twenty men. One has an axe that he waves above his head. He is chopping a length of polished wood as though it were a stick of firewood.

'That is the communion rail,' Father says, flinging open the window.

'Stop, man!' he yells. 'STOP! In the name of God, STOP!'

The man with the axe looks round and laughs and I see that it is the same man who threw a book at Father's head – Isaac Clegg, the fuller.

'I act on orders, Reverend Sir,' he shouts defiantly, hurling a length of the rail into the fire.

'On whose orders?' Father yells.

'Orders of Parliament!' the man shouts back. 'There are to be no more popish practices now that Parliament is recalled.' Another man walks towards the flames and throws an armload of books into them. I see charred flakes dance in the air like birds.

'They must be stopped,' my father says. 'God in heaven! Such desecration of sacred things!' He is buttoning his

47

coat, making as if to leave the room, but my mother, placing herself between him and the door, begs him to stay.

'How can they be stopped?' she says, grabbing him by both arms. 'Half the town is there. The tanner and the smithy and the apothecary and John Sowerby the dyer and all his five sons. You are one man against a mob. They will not listen to you . . .'

Father is pulling away, shaking free of her grasp.

'You will be like Daniel in the den of lions,' Mother says, plucking at his sleeve.

'Then God shall protect me, as he protected Daniel,' says Father.

Mother lets go of him now, and placing her hands on her belly – as though the unborn child would echo her concerns – she sinks into a chair.

'It is an abomination!' Father roars. 'Such wanton destruction! I cannot stand by and let it happen.' And with this he strides from the room. I have never seen my father so angry. Margaret, unnaturally still now beside me, slips her hand into mine and grips it tightly, while my mother weeps quietly in her chair.

I go again to the window and lean out on the sill, Margaret clutching at my skirt. Down below, Father is marching towards the fire with a leather pail. Without warning he sluices water on to the flames and I hear them hiss and spit. But the fire is too big for so little an amount of water and so a gale of contemptuous laughter goes up from the crowd that makes my face burn with shame.

'Will you try to put out the fires of hell also, Reverend Fowler?' one of the men says sarcastically.

'They make a mockery of Father,' I say. 'How dare they treat him like this? They deserve to be in the stocks, every last one of them.'

Father is remonstrating with Isaac Clegg but I cannot hear what he is saying because of the din of voices and the raging of the fire. He waves his arms and wags his finger but to no avail.

Then Margaret gasps with horror.

'Look!' she says. I follow her gaze and see a burly man coming out of the church with Father's golden cope in his arms. He carries it, hooked across the crook of his elbows as though it were a fainted girl, and then, with a mocking bow, he spreads his arms and flings it on to the bonfire.

'Holy God,' says Tabitha, under her breath, as the golden cloth shrinks and crumples into the flames, folding in upon itself, blackened and smoking. 'Has it come to this?'

*

It is several hours before the fuss and the flames die down but by nightfall the street is quiet again, the only trace of the fire a heap of smoking soot no bigger than a molehill. Margaret sleeps closer to me than usual in our bed, and from her tossing and whimpering I suspect that she is dreaming troubled dreams. I lie awake for some time, hearing the church clock strike midnight. Then, as I finally begin to drift into sleep, I hear footsteps on the stairs. Wriggling free of Margaret's thrashing limbs, I creep out of my room and see Father making his way downstairs fully clothed, cloak and hat and everything.

'Father,' I say in a whisper. 'Where are you going at this time?'

'Ssh, child!' he says softly. 'Go back to your bed.'

But I do not go back to bed. I dress myself and follow him.

He goes into the church through the west door. I creep inside and hide quietly in the shadows, my heart thumping in my chest for dread of what I may find. Father and three other men are standing beside the font. They are holding candles and in the soft glow I can see that they are staring upwards.

Above the stone font, seated on its rim, is a tall conical cover made of carved oak. It stretches up, like a pointing finger, taller than two men, rising in a spike towards the vaults of the roof. The carvings that adorn the sides of this tower of oak depict scenes from the lives of the saints – St Paul falling from his horse on the Damascus road, St Stephen being stoned to death, Mary cradling the infant Jesus, St Peter escaping from prison, led by the hand by a liberating angel. I have often looked at these ancient pictures – stroked my hand across the grainy wood to read its stories. This wooden cover is fastened to the ceiling by a chain, rigged, mysteriously, with some sort of pulley. When Father baptizes babies – as he baptized my sister Martha two years past – he lifts the huge cover free of the font and it hangs, suspended a yard or so above his head. Father says this has to do with the balance of lead weights but when I was smaller I thought it miraculous – like Jesus walking on the water.

The men, their faces inclined towards the ceiling, are murmuring to one another. My eyes, adjusting now to the gloom, follow the font cover upwards to the tip of its point where an iron ring attaches it to the supporting chain. Here, I suddenly notice someone at the top of a ladder uncoiling a length of rope. There is a rattle of chains and a shout and then the four men circle the font, setting their candles on the floor, and wrap their arms around the base of the cover as it topples sideways. With much heaving and staggering and swaying the men lower the mighty piece of oak to the ground, where it lies like a felled tree. One of the four then opens the church door to its fullest extent and a fifth man, who appears to have been waiting outside, backs in a horse-drawn wagon. I have never seen a horse in church before and am amazed at such a sight in the dead of night! With more pulling and lifting and hauling on ropes, the font cover is eventually lifted on to the back of the wagon where the weight of it makes the wagon's timbers sag and sway.

Then, as the horse – struggling with its heavy load – plods out through the door, Father sees me lurking beside the wall. I hold my breath, fearing his wrath, but he speaks kindly.

'Grace!' he says, in surprise. 'I told you to go to bed.'

'Forgive me, Father. I could not sleep.'

'Go home. This is no place for a child.' Father's face is grave.

51

'This is the house of God, Father,' I say.

'It is not safe,' he replies.

'Where are they taking it?' I ask, my eyes following the lumbering cart.

'To a place where the barbarous rabble will not find it,' he says.

He takes my arm and leads me towards the door.

'Come, Grace. Home!' A gentleman holds the door open and we step through.

'Thank you, sir,' Father says, and I turn and recognize Thomas Sunderland – the man with the angel above his door.

Abigail

William was pleased when news reached us of the bonfire in the churchyard.

'Praise the Lord!' he said gleefully. He was threading the handloom, winding the warp backwards and forwards across its frame.

'It's as the Parliament has decreed,' he said. 'There are to be no more idols, no graven images, no holy relics, no superstitious pictures – nothing to stand between us and the risen Christ. And no fences, neither – to keep us from the presence of God.'

'You are becoming quite the preacher, William,' my mother said, twisting wool on to a spindle. 'Soon *you* will be the vicar of Middleholme!'

'We are a priesthood of all believers, Mother,' he said. 'There are some that say we have no need of priests at all – that we are all equal, all filled with the Holy Spirit.'

'There are some that talk a lot of nonsense, son,' Mother said, with a weary sigh. 'Let Parliament concern itself with lifting these taxes that squeeze us till we're half blue. And let you concern yourself with weaving kerseys.' She hooked a stray wisp of hair behind her ears and set the spindle on the bench. 'Come on, Abigail,' she said, 'that wool won't card itself!'

*

I thought that day how much I missed my brother Oliver – whose laughter was like leaven in the lump – now that he was so often gone to Saltley Hall. Without his wit and high spirits – the way he'd sometimes make a puppet from a rag and spoon and with it, tell a tale – our household seemed the heavier. My brother William, without his younger brother's taunts and jibes to check him, seemed to lean more to one side, to lose his balance like a stake set on a muddy slope.

*

William was eight years old when I was born. I remember him skinny as a sapling with restless energy like a mill race or a raging fire. Always wanting more. Always wanting to change things. Reverend Jagger, who was the vicar of Middleholme before Grace Fowler's father's time, recognized some spark in William and taught him to read.

'Faith comes by hearing,' he said, 'and hearing by the Word of God. You must read the Scriptures for yourself, William, so that you can hear God's word.'

William mastered his letters quickly and in time taught Father to read, who then taught Oliver and me – though I confess I read slowly and haltingly and Oliver, when he was younger, had not the concentration, given to dreaming as he was. My mother, like many of the spinners and weavers hereabouts, cannot read at all.

It had been William's idea to install a second loom in the workshop, Candlemas before last, so that he and Father could weave at the same time and produce twice as much cloth. William had ambitions. He wanted to build an empire of wool as the Sunderland family had done. To have a booth at Bartholomew Fair in London and to sell our cloth to the four corners of the earth.

'If we employ cottagers to do the carding and spinning, we could make four kerseys in a week, not one,' he said one night when we had eaten supper, 'more, if Oliver will weave, too!'

Oliver, sitting on a stool stitching the pony's broken harness with a stout needle, shrugged and said nothing.

'Why would we employ cottagers to do the work that Abigail and I can do ourselves?' Mother said sceptically.

'So you could do the cropping and finishing,' William said. 'Abigail is skilled with the cropping shears. If our broadcloths were better finished, they would fetch a higher price.' Father had nodded his head and smiled to himself and fondled the top of my head with pride. How different our fortunes might have been if neighbour had not gone to war against neighbour, brother against brother.

*

Barely two years from that night, in the winter I was eleven, William cut his nut-brown hair short above his ears so that he looked like an acorn turned upside down. Oliver, arriving at the our door holding the reins of a beautiful grey horse and a side of ham (the horse from Sir James's stables, the

55

bacon from the larder of Saltley Hall), exclaimed when he saw William's shorn head.

'Good God!' he said. 'You look like a Roundhead! You had better keep your hat on or the King may cut off your ears.' Oliver leaned on the doorpost, flicking his own hair as a horse may shake its mane, but William was unamused.

'The King had better look to his own affairs,' William said. 'They say he has fled from London and is hiding at Hampton Court.'

'Not hiding, Will,' said Oliver. 'Levying troops to defeat the Puritans!'

'Thomas Sunderland says the streets of London are awash with troops – gunners on every corner and armed ships under London Bridge. All ready to defend the rights of Parliament.' William waggled his cropped head, delightedly.

'I reckon he exaggerates,' said Oliver. The grey horse, impatient at standing still, began to snort and paw the ground with its hoof.

'And will you fight for the King, Oliver? You and all Sir James's grovelling servants?' Oliver didn't answer.

'Pah!' said William, turning his back on him. 'You can keep your ham, little brother. I'll not eat food from a Royalist's kitchen!'

'Be quiet, William Booth,' my mother growled, pushing past him to snatch the ham. 'The food is very welcome, Oliver. Please thank her ladyship most kindly.'

*

William never liked Grace Fowler. He said she was full of affectations – frivolous and vain.

'She's not your sort, Abigail,' he said, stuffing wool into a sack. 'Not our sort. She'll make trouble for you.'

At first our friendship was a secret. Grace would wait for me on the wall or watch from her window on market day and – when I could – I'd steal away from cloth or wool or sacks of corn to be with her. Sometimes she'd write a note with ink and paper her father gave her and hide it in a crack in the wall. I'd pull it out as I passed by and slowly decipher her words: 'Meet me on the Hill of the Angels at four strikes of the clock.' But things rarely stay secret in a town like Middleholme.

When Oliver went to work for Sir James Hallam he didn't live at Saltley Hall at first but stayed at Top Slack, rising early to walk down into the valley and out again. For a time he still did what he could, digging the oat field and feeding the animals and – in summer – cutting the hay. But little by little the jobs he'd formerly done became mine. I was strong for my age and lifting sacks of oats or bundles of brushwood was not difficult for me. Though arduous, my new role had advantages. Two or three times a week I'd take the pony into town to fetch or trade things, delighted at the new freedom this gave me and the greater opportunities to see my friend. It was on one such day – a wet grey day in November, when the hills were wrapped in fog – that a girl in a hooded cloak came running towards me on Westgate Street. I was outside the maltster's house, having just exchanged a dozen eggs for a bushel of malt. It was only when she pulled down her hood, revealing her barley straw hair, that I realized it was Grace.

'Abigail, come!' she said. 'I saw you from the window. Come and see. It's terrible. They are smashing things again.' She pulled at my sleeve in an agitated fashion so I hitched the pony to a post beside the maltings and ran with Grace back towards the churchyard.

'I heard the bangs and went to the window,' she said. 'Father had locked the church and barred the way but they smashed the locks and kicked open the door. Then, they carried out the statue of Mary and dashed it to pieces.' Grace talked breathlessly as we hurried across Market Bridge. 'Now they are rampaging in the churchyard,' she said, 'like crazed beasts – destroying statues, carvings, even gravestones – anything they can find.'

As we got closer to the churchyard I could hear the sound of hammers on stone – not the regular, orderly tapping of stone carvers' hammers but a chaotic cacophony of blows – wild and destructive. There used to be a tall angel carved on a headstone beside the south wall. I had, since I was small, been in the habit of admiring it as I passed – marvelling at the golden colour of its stone and the way it seemed to hover there, blessing the grave. Now, when I saw it, I let out a great wail for it had been horribly broken – its wings hacked off and its face pounded and crushed to dust.

'Why would they do this?' Grace cried, reaching her hand out towards the injured angel, her eyes full of tears.

'They think we worship them as idols,' I said. 'Like the Israelites with the golden calf.'

'Do *you* think that, Abigail?' Grace said accusingly.

'Of course not,' I said.

We were at the south gate of the churchyard by then. The sound of the hammer blows had stopped but now we could hear loud voices. Suddenly, through the gateway four men emerged from the fog, hammers in hands. One of them, with whom I now came face to face, was my brother William, his roundhead hair soaked with rain. He looked from me to Grace – her face white with appalled surprise – and back to me.

'Abigail,' he said. 'Go home.' Then he stared darkly at Grace and said, 'Miss Fowler, I don't think you fit company for my sister. I think you'd be wise to go back to the priest's house and bar the doors!' He laughed harshly.

Neither of us moved.

'Well, off you go then, lass,' William said, roughly pushing my shoulder. He was showing off in front of the other men – seeming to bully me and treat me harshly. For all his fiery words William had never been unkind to me.

'I need to fetch the pony,' I said, tears pricking in my eyes. 'From the maltster's house.'

'Well, be quick about it,' he said, pushing me again. 'Or Father will beat you for wasting time.'

'And won't he beat you for desecrating graves?' Grace said boldly. Too boldly, I fear. The men were incensed. Sam Sowerby, who was standing on William's left side with a swaggering look, swung his arm and clipped her across the head with a smack of his palm.

That was when we ran. Grace snatched my hand and pulled me, running, into the vicarage garden and up the path to the house. Opening the front door she pushed me inside and slammed the door behind us.

'Does your face sting? From the slap of his hand?' I asked, hardly able to look at her for shame. Grace took a lock of my wet hair between her finger and thumb.

'Will you be beaten for being my friend?' she asked earnestly.

'I may,' I said. 'But I would bear it gladly.' I raised my eyes to meet hers. Grace smiled at me and I felt myself flood with light as though the sun had broken from the clouds.

*

We waited inside the Fowlers' house for some time before venturing out again. I was relieved to find the pony still tethered and our bushel of malt strapped safely to his back. Yet more relieved, however, was I to find — amidst the wreckage of broken stone that lay about the streets of Middleholme — that Thomas Sunderland's angel, smiling from the lintel above his door, was quite unharmed.

*

Perhaps I made too light of my brother's words about the company I kept. I had no thought to give up my friend, though perhaps from then I learned new secrecy. Grace and I climbed the hill together that afternoon, taking the west route via Coldwater Dene to avoid passing Top Slack for fear that William may see us and stop us in our tracks. I wanted to take some gift to atone for the damage done, to recompense the wounded angel with her severed wings and her battered face – to make some sacrifice for the violence of my brother.

But when we reached the Winstone Rocks the angels were not there. Rain was streaming down the walls of the cave, and beneath where the bright forms usually danced was a great puddle of water.

'The angels are weeping for the broken stones,' Grace said. 'We must leave our gifts, even though they are not here. Then they will know that we are faithful and that we weep, too.' I took a scrap of sheep's wool from my pocket – warm from my fingers playing with it as I climbed the hill – and laid it on the wet rock. Then Grace took a feather from under her cloak. It was the most beautiful feather I had ever seen – green and gold and the deepest blue – with a huge unblinking eye at the tip of it.

'Here is a peacock's feather,' Grace said, softly, 'as a sign that we are sorry.'

Grace

It is a day of torrential rain, the day in March when my mother's child is born — as wet as though some great dam has burst in the heavens. I am in an upstairs room, charged with the care of Margaret and Martha. The rain drums so loudly upon the roof that it muffles the screams that come from the room below where the midwife mixes her herbs and spices. Looking from the window, I see water sluicing down the lane beside the church, flowing in such quantities that it seems as though our house might float away like a boat. Streams are gushing everywhere, pouring off the hillside, whipped white like ribbons. Martha is fractious and unsettled. I rock her in my lap and tell the story of Noah and his ark and the rain that lasted forty days and forty nights.

'Will it rain for forty days in Middleholme?' Margaret asks.

'I hope not,' I say.

As the clock strikes three Tabitha comes in to tell us we have another sister and that her name is Ellen. Presently we file in to peep at her, swaddled in her cradle in a cocoon of cloths.

*

The next day Father lifts me into Falcon's saddle and I ride with him to Saltley Hall where Lady Hallam receives us in a room with beautiful green chairs. Her servant brings Father a cup of wine, from which I am allowed a tiny sip, and some almonds in a silver dish.

'Thanks be to God that Mrs Fowler is safely delivered,' says Lady Hallam. 'And the child healthy and with all its limbs.'

'Thanks be to God indeed,' says Father. 'And grateful thanks also to your ladyship for so generously engaging so able and so cheerful a midwife, on my wife's behalf.'

'It does not do to have a woman attended by the drunk or ignorant, Reverend Fowler. It is a pleasure to provide your wife with this small comfort.' Lady Hallam stands and walks towards me with the dish of almonds. She smiles at me and I reach out my hand to take one.

'And a wet nurse?' she continues. 'Has she now engaged a wet nurse?'

'She has indeed,' my father says.

'And the child's name is to be what?'

'Ellen, your ladyship. My wife's sister's name.'

'It is a good name,' she says with a nod of her head. 'What a pity the child was not a son, Reverend Fowler. But at least a girl will not grow up to be a soldier and fight.' She walks to the window and touching the pane with her finger gazes out across the parkland.

'I see Sir James's troops are now mustering in force,' my father says. On our way here, as Falcon trotted up the gravel drive, we passed a group of foot soldiers plunging their pikes, one by one, into a haystack in the middle of the field. Most of them were just boys, with faces no more bearded than mine.

'You will have heard, no doubt, that the King has established his court at York. Sir James hopes to levy a hundred infantry and a regiment of some three hundred horse. They will fight under the Saltley coat of arms, may God protect them.' She turns from the window, takes a nut from the dish and stands for a moment, lost in thought.

*

On our way back down the drive we see two dozen cavalry soldiers galloping across Saltley Park with drawn swords. Reaching the edge of the wood they turn and trot back towards us and I see that one of them is Oliver, Abigail's brother – the one who reunited me with Lady Hallam's pony, the one with eyes like a morning sky.

*

Riding from the gates of Saltley Hall we descend the hill to the valley bottom. Here, where the River Lumley winds past a row of cottages, we see that the waters have breached their banks and mud is swilling all across our path. The river has a brown, swollen look and all along its margins branches and debris have been deposited as the water level has subsided. When we reach the West Bridge, that sits just downstream of the confluence of the Lumley and the Lusk, we find that the floods have all but destroyed it – washing its stones into the streambed. Samuel, the red-haired stonemason's boy, is there, his legs submerged in the murky water, hauling lumps of rock from the river bottom.

Father reins in his horse and speaks to him.

'That's arduous work for a boy, Samuel,' Father says. Samuel blushes when he sees me and tips his hat.

'I'm sixteen years old now, sir,' says Samuel. 'I'm old enough to fight.'

'And will you fight, Samuel?' Father asks.

'Aye, sir. I'll fight.'

'Will you fight for the King?'

'No, Reverend Sir,' Samuel says, dipping his hands in the flowing stream. 'For Parliament.'

*

In the corner of the churchyard Old Tristram sits with his tin bowl.

'A day of darkness is coming,' he says as we pass. 'When the moon shall fall down from the sky and the streets shall run with blood.' I wrap my arms more tightly around my father's waist and press my face against his coat, inhaling its comforting smell. As we dismount from the horse and walk towards the house, I hear my baby sister cry like a mewling kitten.

Abigail

As a child of twelve I did not believe – despite the arguments between my brothers, and the boiling tempers in the churchyard, and all the dark mutterings about taxes – that war would truly come or that my brothers – my own flesh and blood – would fight bitterly one against the other.

'Why would neighbours go to war – and blast one another with gunpowder and slice one another's limbs with swords and spill blood until there was no more blood left to spill – all because one cuts his hair short while another leaves his long? Because one lights a candle and another prays in a bare room? Because one addresses God in Latin and another in his common tongue? Or one likes black when another likes gold? It is madness! It is as foolish as killing because one man likes cheese when another prefers bacon!'

I shouted my outraged questions to the rocks, to the trees, to the rabbits on the moors, to the bales of cloth heaped on the pony's back – to anything – because no person would listen to me. It felt as though the whole world had gone deaf and taken leave of its senses. Even my father – who thinks that God is good and men are good, and who would, at first, speak ill neither of the King nor of his troublesome Parliament — began to talk as though war was coming as surely as a boulder rolls down a hill.

So it was, in my thirteenth year, that Oliver, himself only sixteen, joined the Royalist army of Sir James Hallam and William enlisted with a band of Parliamentarian militia — a ragtag troop of dyers and croppers whose commander was a clothier from Lumley Bridge. By then, Parliament had seized the port of Hull and King Charles — so William crowingly told us — had failed to recapture it and all the great pile of weapons and gunpowder that were held there. Then there was a battle somewhere called Edgehill. Oliver said that the King had won the battle but William said it was a victory for Parliament because the King had fled to Oxford. King and Parliament. They were just words with no more meaning than clanging bells or the cawing of crows. Yet they divided us, flesh from flesh.

William said that the siege at Hull was a triumph that would stop the King in his tracks but Mother said it would be our ruin. With Hull shut off and no ships leaving the port there was no route out of the county for our wool. Within weeks, the scores of cloth merchants that had thronged the marketplace in Middleholme dwindled to a handful of traders and the price we could fetch for our broadcloth sunk so low we could barely afford to eat.

'When we're all dead from hunger none of us will care what clothes the priest wore or how he said his prayers,' my mother said, stirring pottage over the fire.

*

In that year, the year my brothers became soldiers, lines were being drawn all across the town and countryside, which – though invisible – were as substantial as the racing streams that criss-crossed the moors. Some stood on one side of the line. Some stood on the other. Sir James and Lady Hallam were for the King. So were all their tenant farmers, their servants, and the cottagers that lived on their land. So were the blacksmith and the apothecary, and the strap maker and the maltster. And Thomas Sunderland's three sons and Henry Sowerby, the dyer's son – but not his brother Sam. Some were loyal to the King himself but most were loyal to Sir James or too fearful to set themselves against him. And some just loathed Isaac Clegg and his violent tongue.

Sam Sowerby was for Parliament. And so were the Cleggs from Coldwater fulling mill, and Elijah Woodfield the brewer and Joseph Sutcliffe the tanner and Annie Cropshawe the midwife and most of the weavers and spinners and dyers. And most of the cloth merchants, too. The Reverend Robert Fowler and his wife and daughters were, of course, for the King and we, the Booth family – we were split asunder. Mother said she was for the King – because she could not think ill of Lady Hallam – and Father, reluctantly, was for Parliament because he believed himself more Puritan than Papist. I was for no one. Only for peace.

*

The summer I was thirteen was a terrible summer. It rained and rained and the hills were clamped in cloud for weeks on end. The hay crop rotted in the field, there was so much water, and our poor cow drowned in the beck. Oliver was living at Saltley now, and William – though not yet engaged in fighting – was scarcely ever at Top Slack – what with his marching and musket practice and all his rebel talk. With both my brothers absent from the farm the shearing of the sheep fell to Father and me, and Mother – left to card and spin and wash and crop the wool single-handedly – became quite thin from work and worry. William's loom – but two summers in the workshop – now stood idle, gathering dust, for it was all we could do now to make *one* kersey in a week. To make matters worse, Father's eyesight began to fail him so that, squint as he might over his weaving, he struggled to see the warp threads. At night-time, after working long hours over the loom, he'd clasp his head to relieve the throbbing ache there. Mother would soak a cloth in sage water and press it on his temples.

'It's as if fuller's hammers were pounding in my skull,' he'd say.

Then, on the first day of July, word came of a battle less than a day's march away from Middleholme. I was at the forge of Nathan Horsfall the blacksmith early in the morning, when Henry Sowerby burst in.

'There's been fighting,' he said, 'on the moors the other side of Bradford. Dozens of men are dead. Some from Middleholme, so they say.'

It had been more than a week since we'd seen either William or Oliver.

'*Who* is dead?' I said. '*Who*, from Middleholme?' A sudden cold dread shot through me despite the outer heat of the forge.

'Elijah Woodfield, for one,' said Henry, 'and the maltster's boy and Annie Cropshawe's son, too ...'

'And my brothers?' I said.

'Don't know, Miss,' Henry Sowerby said.

'And is the battle over?' Nathan Horsfall asked, pausing in his work, a red-hot horseshoe glowing on the anvil.

'Aye,' said Henry, 'and the Puritan rebels are routed – outnumbered by Sir James's troops. I heard tell that most of the Parliamentarian soldiers are now all fled and that Middleholme is all for the King again.'

*

I hurried home with the news and Mother, on hearing that there had been a battle, turned white as linen. Father set to praying, muttering incessantly as he worked the loom, and I – leaving my fleeces for an hour in the middle of the day – ran to the Winstone Rocks to beg the angels to watch over my warring brothers. Grace's peacock feather was still there on the floor of the cave, glinting gold where the sun streamed through the rock and illuminated it. I prayed that somehow both my brothers were living and well and that word would come soon of their safety.

*

The very next evening Joseph Crabtree rode to Top Slack from Lumley Bridge to tell us that William was unharmed and had gone into hiding in Lancashire with the rebel army. Mother was so grateful for the news that she gave Joseph Crabtree the last of our bread so that I went to bed hungry. But despite the pangs of my belly my heart was glad.

The following morning I took our strip of kersey to the fulling mill at Coldwater Dene. As I approached the mill race, I noticed that the normal thumping sound of the fulling stocks was missing and that the valley was strangely quiet. When I reached the mill I discovered there was nobody there and the rollers and beaters and water wheel were all quite still and silent. Retracing my steps I ran into Joseph the stonemason who told me that Isaac Clegg and his sons were turned tail and fled to Rochdale, and that his wife Sarah and her three daughters were vanished into thin air.

By afternoon the King's soldiers had poured into Middleholme and the streets were thronging with troops, some of them injured but all of them in good spirits. Then, just as the sun was going down, there was a knock at our door. Father opened it warily, for fear of bad news, and there – alleluia – was my brother Oliver, smiling. I rushed to embrace him, his soldier's tunic rough against my skin.

'God be praised,' my mother said, wiping oatmeal from her hands. She pressed him to sit by the fire and to drink a cup of ale with us. Oliver was full of the King's victory and of how the cavalry troops had routed Fairfax's foot soldiers, riding at them from two sides.

'Fairfax's men were a hopeless rabble,' he said. 'Some were so drunk they could barely stand to fight, and dozens of them fled the field.'

'And did you see William?' Father said.

'William?' my brother said. 'Did he fight with the Puritans?'

'I believe so,' Father said.

'And is he well?' Oliver asked, his face softening with concern.

'We are told so,' Father said. 'He too is fled – though not, I'm sure, from cowardice.'

'Well,' said Oliver, hardening his face again, 'pray God he sees the error of his ways and supports the King again, now that Parliament's soldiers are defeated.' With that he drained the last drop of ale from his cup and left, riding off into the gloom.

*

Within days there were several hundred soldiers in Middleholme. A regiment of cavalry was posted on the hill at Saltley Gap to guard the route down the valley to Lumley Bridge. Those who had supported Parliament and spoken against the King fell silent and lived in fear of their lives. There were rumours of skirmishes on the moors, women used roughly and farms ransacked. My mother, visiting the wise woman for some remedy for Father's poor throbbing head, learned that Sarah Clegg was hiding at the house of Annie Cropshawe the midwife near Blackwater Clough.

'She and her three bairns all given refuge, God bless Annie Cropshawe's soul,' my mother said, setting down her basket of herbs on the oak table. I was pouring milk from an earthenware jug that was heavy in my hands.

'And her poor husband,' my mother continued, 'Isaac Clegg – loud, axe-wielding Puritan that he was – trying to reach her and his daughters under cover of night, seized by soldiers – God have mercy – and his throat slit like a butchered lamb.'

When my mother said this, the sight of Isaac Clegg's red face drained of blood flashed before my eyes and the earthenware jug slipped from my hands and smashed on the stone floor.

Grace

Ellen, my baby sister, is sick. She cries unceasingly and thrashes her hot limbs. Her eyes run and her nose is crusted with green slime. She has grown more sick with each hour of the day and now night has come and my mother is at her wit's end with worry and exhaustion – besides which she is expecting another child and vomits often into a pail. I pity her and hope that I shall never marry or bear children. Father has been called out to baptize a sick child, lest she die unblessed and go to hell. (I do not like to think a child may go to hell but Father says we are all sinners and all stand in need of the Holy Sacraments – even babies.)

'Why cannot he stay?' my mother says, exasperated, 'and tend his own sick child!' Tabitha brings water in a bowl and a rag to soak Ellen's forehead. Margaret and Martha are asleep in a bed in the corner of the parlour. The room upstairs where the three of us used to sleep has three soldiers in it now. Three more are billeted in the room where Father and Mother used to sleep. Tabitha is ragged with the extra mouths to feed and with their clamouring for ale and hot water to wash in and bread and more meat. Father says he is glad of them in the town and that God is to be thanked for defending us from the Puritan rabble. They are the King's troops and welcome as honoured guests. Tabitha says if they are the King's troops then the King should pay for their pies and puddings.

Mother wants medicine from the apothecary for Ellen's fever but Tabitha is too busy to go.

'I'll fetch it,' I say, and I put on my shawl.

*

It is a warm night and dark with the lack of a moon. I walk quickly down the lane past the churchyard and on to Market Bridge. I can hear the river gurgling underneath and – my eyes adjusting now to the darkness – I stop to look down at the black water. As I cross the market square a group of soldiers pass by and one of them whistles at me, the way a man will whistle for his dog.

The apothecary's shop is in South Street but, the shop now being long closed, I turn down the alleyway that runs around the back. It is even darker here and I must use the touch of my fingertips to feel my way along the slippery passageway. Reaching a door I knock loudly with my knuckles and a woman calls out, 'Who's there?'

'Grace Fowler,' I say.

'The shop's closed,' she shouts back.

'Please help me,' I call. 'My sister is sick.'

She opens the door and peers at me, waving a lighted candle in my face.

'Who did you say you are?' she says.

'Grace Fowler, mistress,' I say. 'My father is the priest.'

She opens the door a little wider and beckons me inside with a nod. Leading me through into the murky shop she gives me a jar of powder.

'Wintergreen and angelica,' she says, and I hand her the coins my mother has given me.

I put the jar into my pocket and fumble my way back down the passageway to South Street. But just as I reach the lane, two soldiers appear and block my path. One draws his sword and stretches it across the alleyway to bar my way.

'Stop!' he says fiercely and then he laughs raucously and his friend laughs, too. I make to pass them but he keeps his sword across the passageway.

'Not so fast,' he says. His friend steps towards me and, seizing my chin in his hand, tilts my face upwards, the better to see me.

'It's late to be walking the streets, isn't it?' he says. 'Especially for one so young. And so pretty.' He lets go of my chin and I make to pass them again. But this time the first soldier, sheathing his sword, grabs me by the shoulders.

'Let me go,' I say, attempting to shake myself free. 'My sister is sick. She needs medicine.'

'And we need company,' the first soldier says. He runs his hand roughly through my hair so that it snags and tugs — the way it does when Mother brushes it too hastily.

'Please,' I say, 'I must get home.'

'Surely you can spare a minute for a pair of brave soldiers,' the second one says, catching me round the waist.

76

'Leave me, I beg you,' I say, struggling to get free. 'I'm for the King!'

'I'm pleased to hear it,' says the first soldier, clasping my wrists and pushing me up against the wall.

Before I can protest he kisses me. His hot whiskery mouth smells of ale and onions. I push and kick to be free of his embrace but he only grips me harder.

'Leave her!' someone shouts, and the soldier momentarily loosens his grip. Through the darkness I can just make out another soldier on a horse. I try to wriggle free and make a dash but the soldier who has kissed me seizes me again and wraps his big arms around me so that I am pinned like a post. The other soldier now draws his sword and points it towards the man on the horse.

'Let her go,' the soldier on horseback says again.

'What's the matter?' says the soldier with the sword. 'Do you want her for yourself?'

The soldier holding my arms laughs darkly and I feel his chest heave against me.

'She's only a child,' the soldier on the horse says.

'She's old enough to make a soldier happy,' the soldier with the sword says. 'So you'll have to fight us for her!'

Instantly, the third soldier dismounts from his horse and strikes the soldier with the sword across the head with the butt of his musket. The soldier who kissed me now lets go of my arms and leaps to defend his injured friend but before he can unsheathe his sword the cavalryman kicks him so hard that he falls to the ground with a grunt.

I stand in the lane, stiff with fright, not sure which way to run – but before I can run anywhere the cavalryman grabs me and thrusts me on to his horse. Then, swinging into the saddle behind me he kicks the horse and it canters down South Street. The horse does not stop but crosses the market square and over Market Bridge into the lane beside the church. Passing the churchyard the soldier rides right into the vicarage garden and, slipping from the saddle, deposits me at my door.

'How did you know where I live?' I say, my heart still racing with fear. He does not speak but removes his helmet so that I can make out the contours of his face. It is Oliver Booth.

'Thank you,' I say, catching my breath. 'I am very grateful to you.'

'You're welcome,' he says and he bows extravagantly. I wonder if he is mocking me and feel myself blush scarlet. He holds my gaze a moment, smiling. Then, putting his helmet back on and remounting his horse he says, 'Goodnight,' and leaves.

Abigail

The King's soldiers stayed in Middleholme all through the summer into the autumn and all through the winter until the snow was thick on the ground. My brother Oliver came back to live at Top Slack, along with three other cavalrymen – one of whom, Tobias, was a drunken lout. Oliver had grown rough and careless in their company and I was dismayed by the lack of respect with which he spoke to our father. Since their job was soldiering – 'defending Middleholme from the Roundhead brigands', Oliver said – they did nothing to help with sheep or cloth making. And yet they ate our food, faster than we could produce it. Even their horses – two of which were procured ('stolen', my father said) from neighbouring farms – ate our hay, precious little though we had of it. By Christmas time we had slaughtered most of our sheep and all but two of our chickens, and the pig which we killed at All Hallows – and which would normally have seen us right through the winter months – was all eaten up by the Feast of St Nicholas. It was a struggle to find enough food for seven of us. Father taught me to snare rabbits on the hill and to strangle the life out of them when I found them thrashing in the traps. Mother taught me to skin them and scrape their hides. I sold the skins to the glove maker on Westgate Street and spent the money on flour and cheese.

*

After the death of Isaac Clegg – or 'murder', as many called it out of earshot of the soldiers, for there were some now who were calling him 'a martyr to the Puritan cause' – the fulling mill at Coldwater Dene fell into disrepair. Taking our cloth to be fulled at the mill on the other side of the valley took three times as long, and collecting it again from the tenter fields was half a day's walk. With William gone from the farm and Oliver as good as absent, and with Father getting blinder by the day, I had to learn to work the handloom. It was hefty work and made my shoulders ache but with our sheep all gone and our food consumed as though a swarm of locusts had passed over us – as in the time of Moses – I knew we must keep weaving kerseys, or surely starve. Mother now took in extra carding and spinning, like a poor cottager, and worked until her fingers were raw. With Hull still held by the King's enemies and few ships able to arrive or leave the port, the only route for cloth traders was overland to London. Thomas Sunderland – may God bless him – continued to buy and sell cloth, carrying it with eight or nine packhorses to his brother Josiah, who had four booths at St Bartholomew's Fair. So we sold our kerseys to him and were glad of whatever price he could give us.

*

After the Battle of Adwalton Moor – the battle just beyond Bradford, where the King's troops had been victorious – I didn't see my brother William for half a year. We missed him – missed his vigour, the loudness of his voice, the sight of his broad back bent over a kersey. Word reached us from time to time that he was in good health.

'Tell him to come home,' my mother said, when Joseph Crabtree greeted her in the Market Square. 'Tell him to forget his fighting and come back to his family. And to his loom!'

Oliver and his soldier friends said the Roundheads were finished and that by the end of the year they would be defeated and all the traitors hanged. But Father – who lately had taken to meeting in secret with dyers and weavers who prayed daily for the time when Puritan armies would free England from Satan's grip – said that the Royalists were losing their hold on the north and that a commander called Oliver Cromwell, who some called 'Ironside', was rallying the cause of Parliament.

'May God prosper them!' he said. Little by little I had seen Father's loyalties shifting, the way a tree set in the prevailing wind will lean gradually more and more in one direction. Mother, still wedded to keeping the peace, scolded as she brushed a length of cloth with a teasel, whispering, 'Hush your treasonous talk, with soldiers in the house.' But Father thumped his fist on the table.

'What?' he said. 'Do you think I am afraid of my own son – and him barely a man – or of his drunken friends?' Father had, through sleeplessness and hunger and the pain in his head, grown more and more short-tempered lately and I feared that he would fight with Oliver – so weary was he of the soldiers and their ill-disciplined ways.

*

In all the long months the King's soldiers were billeted at Top Slack I visited the Hill of the Angels but a handful of times. Still Grace, with no thought of danger, slipped notes in the crack in the wall, but between trapping and weaving and trudging the moors with bundles of cloth I had scarcely an hour to myself.

'The angels need our gifts,' Grace said one rare day as we crouched on the floor of the cave. 'So that they will protect the ones we love.' We'd brought them flowers in summer – wild thyme and yellow irises from the bog beneath the crag. In autumn we'd brought leaves the colour of rust and acorns and horse chestnuts.

'Here is an apple from our tree,' said Grace, smiling as she pulled a round scarlet fruit from her pocket. Once, in winter, we tramped to the Winstone Rocks through deep snow and I gave the angels a jagged ice spear – cold and clear – that I found along the banks of the stream. It was melting from the warmth of my hand as I laid it on the carpet of bracken that Grace had put there in summertime, so that my hand was awash with its tears. The angels weren't there that day. The walls of the cave were blank and grey.

*

One day in January there was a fearful storm and the wind howled and raged around Top Slack. The pony was distressed and, when night fell, I sat with him in the barn for a time to give him comfort. His grey fur was matted with dried mud and as I rubbed him clean with my hand I felt his ribs, poking proud through the skin like bars on a gate.

'Poor Pigeon,' I said, stroking his soft nose. 'Poor hungry Pigeon.'

There was such a constant clatter and flapping from the wind that I did not at first hear the door opening. Nor, with my face pressed up close to the pony's warm nostrils, did I immediately notice that someone was moving about in the barn. But as I came to leave I glimpsed a dark shape and, stopping in my tracks, stood rigid with fear. The shape, preoccupied with searching, or hiding something – I knew not which – in a pile of straw, became suddenly aware of my presence. It stood up from its crouching posture, freezing as a hare will freeze when startled, so that we faced each other as two statues. Then the shape spoke.

'Abigail?' I recognized the voice. It was my brother William. 'Abigail?' he said again. 'Is it you?'

My eyes, adjusting now to the gloom, took him in. Had he not spoken my name I doubt if I would have recognized him, so changed was he in every way. His chest and shoulders, once broad and strong from labour and good food, were scrawny as a goat and his face, once rosy and full, was now quite drawn and sunken. About his chin was a matted beard and his hair was grown so long again that I might have mistaken him for a cavalier. His cheek was bleeding – a trail of wet darkness glistened in a beam of moonlight slipping through the crack in the door. In his arms was a sack that looked, from the way he was holding it, to be exceedingly heavy.

I stretched out my arms to embrace him – scenting his familiar salt smell – but he backed away, clutching his heavy burden to his chest. Unabashed, I stepped forwards and touched his cheek, causing him to flinch in pain.

'You're hurt,' I said. 'Let me bathe it for you.' William ignored my offer.

'So grown,' he said, looking at me.

'You've been gone so long,' I said.

'Father? Mother?' he said, a look of pain tightening across his brow. 'Are they both well?'

'They are living,' I said. 'Too hungry to be called well.' William sighed wearily. He was not yet two and twenty but he seemed an old man.

'The Kingdom of God is coming, Abigail, when there shall be no more hunger and no more tears.' He looked at me and I saw, for a moment, a spark of his old fire.

'May it come soon,' I said.

'And Oliver?' William said. 'Is he living, too?'

'Yes,' I said.

'And still for the King?'

'Yes,' I said.

'And at Saltley?'

'No, he is billeted here – and three more soldiers also,' I said. At this he glanced about him, agitated. Outside the barn a dog barked.

'William, it is not safe for you here,' I said urgently. 'You must not stay.'

84

'I don't mean to stay, lass.' He hesitated, still holding the heavy bundle. Then, stepping towards me he said, 'Sister, if you love me, turn your back and be silent.' So I turned and behind me I heard the rustle of straw. William grabbed my shoulders then and I stiffened again, unsure of what he might do next. Turning me round, like a spindle, he pressed his finger to my lips. 'Say nothing,' he said, 'of what you have seen.'

'Middleholme is for the King and all the supporters of Parliament are fled or silenced—' I said, but William interrupted me, seizing my hands in his.

'But not for long, Abigail. Scottish troops are coming and the King's soldiers are without arms to fight. Just this night a baggage train has been ambushed – pistols and carbines all snatched. The cavaliers will be gone, Abigail, by the end of the month. Mark my words . . .'

'Let me wash your wound before you go,' I said again. 'Or bad humours might infect you.'

'The bad humours are the King's troops – and all their idle popish ways, sister,' he said, with no glimmer of a smile.

As he spoke I heard the sound of a horse's hooves approaching the barn. Then the door opened and my younger brother was standing there, holding the reins of his horse.

When Oliver saw William he drew his sword. In that instant, seeing them on the brink of combat, I remembered them fighting in this barn as boys – rolling in the hay and pummelling one another with their fists.

'My traitorous brother,' Oliver said. 'I could kill you.' He stepped over the threshold.

'And I you,' said William, pulling a pistol from his coat.

Sometimes, when they fought in childhood, Father would clap their heads together like two stones in a river. With all my heart I wished that I might do this now – that they would see sense and beat their weapons into ploughshares. Seeing them so ravaged by war, so twisted with hate, I felt as if *I* might split in two like a tree felled by a fork of lightning.

'Brothers!' I said and I reached a hand out to them both just as I did when they swung me like the church bell.

Oliver sheathed his sword and turned away. William left – slipping off into the night as quickly as he had come. In the morning, creeping in at first light, I searched the barn and found, hidden under a mound of straw, disguised in a bale of wool, a case of pistols and some twenty carbines. The sack, which William had staggered to hold, contained two barrels of gunpowder and a half-dozen musket balls. I hid them again, taking care to conceal them in the wool, and spoke of them to no one – not even Grace Fowler.

*

William was right – prophesying as accurately as if he were Old Tristram. By the time January was out, the King's troops had all left Middleholme and new soldiers clattered into our streets. Roundheads. From Scotland.

Grace

After the King's soldiers leave Middleholme – streaming out of the valley at first light – my sisters and I move back into the upstairs room. I have grown so used to sleeping in the parlour, with the comforting sound of my parents' breathing, that now – this first night in my old bed – I sleep fitfully as cold moonlight streaks in through the window. I hear the clock strike two o'clock, and three o'clock, and four o'clock, too, as I lurch from one nightmare to another. I dream of breaking glass and bleeding hands and severed heads and wake the next morning – my sister Margaret resting in the crook of my arm – bathed in sweat.

Tabitha, returning from the market, brings word from Saltley Hall.

'Roundhead soldiers everywhere, Alice Fry says.' (Alice Fry is her ladyship's kitchen maid.) 'Plundering and rampaging. And Lady Hallam thrown out of her own bed! And she – now that his Lordship Sir James is gone to York with his regiment – all by herself up there, poor soul! And now they are all demanding to be fed – as though we haven't fed soldiers enough!' I worry for Lady Hallam, alone and unprotected, and pray that God will send angels to guard her.

Then I help Tabitha make a currant pie.

I have just finished stirring the pastry when Father comes in, in a terrible state.

'Grace, come quickly and see,' he says, and I follow him, wiping my hands on my skirt as I go. He leads me out of the door of our house and across the churchyard and in through the west door, beside the font. Taking my hand he takes me the length of the nave and then I see and exclaim in horror. Where the stained glass window should be – behind the pulpit, stretching right across the east wall of the church – is a great hole, wide as a gaping mouth. And the coloured glass, smashed to smithereens, is strewn upon the floor like spilled paint. I stoop to look at it, touching the shattered fragments with the toe of my shoe. There is a splinter of blue from the sky and a jagged piece of green from the hills. There is a torn scrap of red from Jesus' cloak and some pearly white from the lamb across his shoulders. There is yellow from his halo – tiny beads of it, like scattered corn. Some pieces are no bigger than my fingernail, some are larger than a book. They are sharp and angry. Bending down, I lift a piece the shape of a pointed shoe – blue as Lady Hallam's peacocks – and look through it at a bleak blue world. Scanning the pieces heaped on the floor I try to reconstruct the picture they once made in my mind's eye but see nothing but a rainbow of rubble. Then, suddenly, among the glassy shards, I spot the face of Jesus and my heart misses a beat. Although his halo is snapped off and his

88

golden hair gone – as though shaved away – his eyes, his nose, his lips, his chin are all there, intact and unharmed. And he is looking at me – imploring me to shelter him. I step across the littered fragments, hearing them crunch underfoot, and pick up the delicate glassy face. It sits on the palm of my hand staring at me, as though I were looking in a mirror or gazing into a pool.

'I am the good shepherd, the good shepherd giveth his life for the sheep,' I say softly, stroking the face's icy smoothness with my thumb.

Father is on his knees picking up daggers of glass and putting them into a wooden pail. I see that his hands are all cut and bleeding.

'Can it be mended?' I say.

'I doubt it,' he says wearily, and I notice that tears have filled his eyes. 'Not while the hearts of men are so hardened with hatred.'

Father has not seen the face in my hand and I am half afraid to show it to him lest, in his despair, he toss it in the pail with all the other broken glass. So I carefully wrap it in my shawl and take it home with me, knowing its wholeness to be a tiny miracle.

Abigail

It was a frosty morning in early February, the sun still rising over the hill behind Blackwater Clough. I was fetching water from the well behind our house, my hands smarting as I broke the crust of ice with a stone. I saw a figure coming up the hill from the town — climbing up the packhorse path, slithering on the cobbles — and watching it as I lowered my bucket, I realized it was Grace Fowler. Leaving the pail beside the well I ran to welcome her.

'I slipped out early, before it was light,' she whispered, glancing about her as though she feared she may have been followed. 'Mother will not let me walk abroad now that the town is full of Roundheads. God knows, she says, the King's soldiers were ruffians but the soldiers of Parliament are all savages!'

I had not seen Grace for several weeks. She looked thinner and paler than before. I bent forward to kiss her forehead and saw that she was holding something in the folds of her skirt.

'Come with me to the Hill of the Angels, Abigail,' she said. 'I have something we must hide there.'

'Show me,' I said but she shook her head.

'Wait till we are safe,' she answered.

I took my pail of water quickly back to Mother, who was struggling to start the fire, and I lied to her – God forgive me – saying that I was going to feed the pony and the chickens. Then I went with Grace Fowler to the Winstone Rocks to the secrecy of our cave.

Once we had both squeezed through the gap in the rocks – a tighter fit now we were both grown taller – and were seated on the cold floor, Grace unwrapped the thing she had been carefully carrying and I saw that it was a face painted on glass – delicate and colourless as a sheet of ice.

'It is Jesus,' she whispered, and at once I recognized it from the stained glass window. Jesus – the Good Shepherd who gathers the lambs in his arms.

I thought immediately of my brother William, talking with fury about the images of Christ in glass and paint and telling us – for now he was eating again at our table and Oliver was gone – how Parliament would cleanse our church from all these 'detestable idols'.

'The windows are all destroyed,' he'd said but a few nights ago, dipping bread into his dish. 'Soon, no pictures – no vain superstitious artefacts – no graven images whatsoever will remain.'

'What harm is there in pictures?' I had asked, fetching a lump of cheese to the table.

'Christ is God and man together,' my father had said. 'Man-made pictures show him as nothing more than flesh. Man but not God. These representations are therefore *mis*representations!' I had not thought Father's mind so fixed and made up. Where was his gentleness? Since the Scottish soldiers had arrived in Middleholme Father had been meeting openly with his company of weavers and dyers to discuss the things of God and he had, from all this fiery talk, grown so fierce in his views that I rarely dared to question him. I could not see how coloured glass might offend God when God himself had created the colours of the chaffinch and the yellowhammer and the spotted wood-pecker. Why might splendour displease one who had made the wing of a butterfly or the back of a ladybird or the purple heather in summer or a meadow in spring?

'They smashed the window all to pieces,' Grace said, stroking her finger over the shard of glass. I nodded, feeling myself blush with shame at the memory of my brother's satisfaction at this act. 'But the face survived unharmed.' She held it up so that rays of light, coming through a chink in the rock, streamed through it and made it gleam.

'It is a miracle,' I said. Grace looked at me, nodding in agreement.

'I am sure of it,' she said. 'It is a sign that all will be well.'

She rested the face against the wall underneath the place where our angels were flickering.

'He will command his angels to guard you in all your ways,' Grace said, quoting the Psalms. I looked at the glass eyes with their gentle, forthright gaze and remembered the whole window – its riot of colour splashed behind the preacher's head.

'It is not safe at home, any more,' Grace said, quickly. 'Soldiers ransack the houses of all and sundry – stripping them of their linen, their tableware, their furniture. Thomas Sunderland's house was plundered and all his silver taken. Father says the Roundheads will exchange it for pistols and gunpowder.'

My mind flashed on the cache of weapons stowed in the barn at Top Slack. After the King's troops left there was much talk of Will's bravery. Of how he and Joseph Crabtree had held up a supply train coming over Blackmoor Top – the carriers of the weapons disguised as wool traders, their pistols and powder concealed in bales of wool strapped to the backs of packhorses. That trickle of blood on his cheek. I wondered what treacherous deeds he had done that he might snatch those weapons.

'My father says the north is falling to Parliament,' Grace said, 'and that soon Fairfax will march on the King's army at York.'

I thought then of my brother Oliver. We had been told that he – and all the Saltley regiment – were gone to York. I recalled how my father had visited York once and told us of its wonderful Minster 'five times bigger than our church at Middleholme and like an apparition of the heavenly city'. I hoped, looking down at the fragment of broken glass that Grace had retrieved, that such a glorious thing as a Minster would not be destroyed.

'The Puritans have daubed all the paintings with black pitch and hacked the statues from the walls of the church as though they were pulling rotten teeth,' Grace said. 'Soon there will be no beauty at all. The church will be like a bare barn. I cannot comprehend it!'

'They believe that true beauty lies in obedience to Scripture,' I said. 'Not in things made by men.'

'You sound like a Puritan, too, Abigail Booth,' Grace said, eyeing me warily. 'Will you stand against King Charles as well?' I was silent for a moment, feeling the weight of my confusion – surrounded as I was, night and day, by Puritan talk which even my mother now showed signs of being swayed by. Eventually I looked straight at Grace and said, 'I will not stand against you.'

Grace fixed me with her stare, unsmiling. 'Nor I against you,' she said.

*

'ABIGAIL!' I heard my brother William angrily shouting my name.

'Abigail!' he roared again. 'Come out here!' I froze with fright, too alarmed to speak. 'We have been followed here,' Grace whispered, crouching low against the wall. When I didn't answer William forced himself into the cave, pushing his way – I cannot think how – through the gap in the rock until he was squeezed in beside us, filling the space. William looked around the cave, waiting for his eyes to adjust to the gloom.

'So this is where you sneak off to secretly with your Papist friend, is it?' I willed him not to see the fragment of stained glass, propped against the wall. Grace, as if reading my thoughts, shuffled sideways so that her body would obscure his view of it but this only made William suspicious.

'What are you hiding, priest girl?' he said rudely, and lurching forward he pushed Grace out of the way.

'Nothing,' Grace said. 'We only come here to play, as children . . .'

But William had seen the glass face – the idolatrous image of Christ – cradled on a bed of bracken and instantly made a grab for it.

'No!' Grace shouted but William snatched it up and dashed it violently against the wall of the cave. I watched as it shattered on to the floor like raindrops. Grace let out a sob but I bit my lip to keep my eyes from filling with tears lest William think me idolatrous, too. His eyes were searching the cave now, taking in the cushion of bracken leaves, the peacock feather, the pearl button, the broken eggshell, the hank of sheep's wool. Shuffling towards the bracken he kicked out with his boot, crushing the blackbird's egg underfoot. Then he picked up the button and hurled it through the gap in the rock. I noticed that the angels – so bright only a moment ago – had completely vanished.

'Witchcraft!' he shouted. 'Has it come to this – my own sister, worshipping the devil?'

'It is not devil worship,' I said. 'It's . . .' Grace was looking at me imploring me not to betray our secret but I said no more because William slapped my cheek to silence me. Then he pulled me by the hair, dragging me roughly from the cave and out on to the cold hillside.

'I forbid you, Abigail,' he said, gripping my arm, 'I forbid you ever to see that Papist witch again! Pray that Christ in his mercy may wash your soul clean from this foulness.'

I did not dare turn back to look at Grace Fowler and William did not release his grip until we were back home at Top Slack. There, Father beat me four times with a leather strap – once for shirking my work, once for lying to my mother, once for worshipping graven images and once – oh, falsehood – for consorting with the devil. Inwardly I smarted with shame to have displeased my dear father so. Never had he whipped me with such vehemence before. I would have sobbed – so distraught was I at being separated from my friend and so roughly handled by my family – but rather, for fear they should interpret any tears as penitence, I stared at the floor and blinked with fury.

Grace

Father wears black now. He looks like a tree in winter. The hole where the stained glass used to be is boarded up with planks so that the church – once flooded with jewelled light – is gloomy and dark. All brightness is gone. There is no colour. There are no candles. Nothing sparkles or shines. When we sing, we sing without musical instruments. Everything is stripped bare and unadorned, as though we were in mourning.

*

In the year that I am fourteen we celebrate Easter on a glorious spring day. In the churchyard there are bright buds and fresh tips of new grass poke through the soil. But inside the church I am reminded more of the tomb than of the glories of the risen Christ. Father, going through the motions of the Mass, has a great weight of sadness about him, as though a heavy chain were wound around his heart.

*

Our garden is abloom with apple blossom and lilac. I pick some and set them in a jug in the parlour. Mother is sewing there. She smiles when she sees the flowers.

'Those are pretty, Grace,' she says. 'They lift my spirits.'

I am glad to have given her joy. Mother's sickness is long past now and her belly swells and ripens like fruit. Her skin has a lustrous glow, as though the baby growing inside her has made her flesh happy. I know that the child is to be born at harvest time. We will carry him to church for baptism like a sheaf of corn. Father and Mother and Margaret and Martha and Ellen and I.

I go into the garden and pick some more blossoms. The apple flowers are rosy white and delicate as baby's fingernails. The lilac — beaded with rainwater and fat as bobbins of wool — are purple, the colour of the amethyst that I have seen about Lady Hallam's neck. Walking through the gate into the churchyard I take the flowers into the church and put them on the altar. I think that God is pleased with them — that they cheer him, as they cheered my mother. That their wetness and the richness of their colour give him joy. I leave them there and tiptoeing through the sanctuary I climb the pulpit steps. I am alone in the church and there is a deep dusty hush. I stand in the pulpit, my hands resting on its cool marble rim and wonder what it feels like for Father to stand here. Many of the congregation, since the Roundheads came, have taken to heckling Father when he preaches. Made bold by the presence of soldiers, their tongues — silenced for so long by the presence of the King's army — now flap like laundry in the wind.

'God is love,' I say to the absent congregation. The words drip from my lips as refreshing as dew.

I am still standing in the pulpit, staring at the empty space, when the west door opens. Afraid at being caught here and thought irreverent, I duck down so that I am concealed by the pulpit's walls. Through the lattice cut in the stonework I see four soldiers walking towards the font, leading a large horse by a rope halter. It is a moment before I realize that the horse is Falcon, Father's chestnut gelding. He wears no saddle and his hooves trail wisps of straw across the stone flags as though he has been brought – this very moment – from his stable at the vicarage. The four soldiers, and the horse, make a circle around the font. I crouch in the pulpit watching the scene unfold.

'Hang on a moment,' one of them says and he goes, alone, to the vestry where Father prepares himself before a service. After a moment the man returns wearing Father's cassock which, on account of Father's tallness and the soldier's stoutness, drags along the floor and cannot be buttoned across the soldier's belly. As well as the cassock, the soldier has two grey stockings dangling from under his hat, like spaniels' ears, which I assume to be in mockery of Father's hair for they are greeted by the others with great mirth. Pulling himself up to his full height this soldier then, in an affected nasal voice, says, 'Do we have godparents?' Whereupon one of the others – a man with a red beard – says, 'Aye, Reverend! I'll be the godfather.' Then the soldier standing next to him – who has a boy's face – produces a shawl and wraps it around his head and says, in a high-pitched voice with much giggling, 'And I, Widow Fowler, I will be the godmother.'

It seems there is to be a baptism but I see no child anywhere. I drop to my knees and press my eye against the marble opening, the better to see the proceedings. The soldier impersonating my father speaks again.

'What name do you give this horse, good friends?'

Now the soldier holding Falcon's halter speaks up. 'His name is Esau,' he says, 'for he is hairy!' There is a great belly laugh from all four soldiers, which holds up their little ceremony for some time. When they have finally recomposed themselves the 'priest', looking into the font, says, 'I fear we have no water.'

At this – and I can hardly bear to look, so crude and sacrilegious is what happens next – the 'godfather' unbuttons his fly and urinates into the font with a great sigh. The laughter that greets this act is even louder than that prompted by the naming of the horse and it resounds so long that I cannot hear the words they speak as they splash the steaming water over the horse's ears. Silence falls, however, as the soldier-priest makes the sign of the cross on Falcon's forehead.

'In the name of the Father, and the Son, and the Holy Spirit . . .' he says in a pompous voice that I realize is supposed to sound like my father. Then with a great slap of the horse's rump and much renewed laughter they turn and lead Falcon away from the font. Just before he reaches the door Falcon lifts his tail and deposits a great pile of dung on the stone flags and the soldiers laugh so loud I think that they will burst.

*

Father boils with fury when I tell him what has happened – though I cannot bring myself to tell him about the red-bearded man passing water into the font. He says that there are some among the Puritans that forbid the baptism of babies and that hold all sacraments in contempt.

'They do not cherish the things that are sacred, Grace,' Father says. He removes his spectacles and pinches the bridge of his nose. 'They think they have no need of a priest. And I fear that those who believe such things are ever growing in number . . .' We are in Father's study, and as he says this I see, outside the window, a great flock of crows rising from a tree.

Abigail

My brother Oliver was never one for strong opinions. Often he would disagree with William but more for the pleasure of provoking him than on account of his convictions. If William was like a thunderstorm – full of rage and fury – Oliver was like a mild summer's day.

As a boy Oliver had an ease about him that I liked. He would daydream his way through his chores, humming to himself as he planted corn or milked the cow or saddled the pony as though a whole world existed in his head that none of us could see. He was playful and agile and good at climbing. Once he climbed right to the top of the sycamore tree behind John Sowerby's house and Mother, coming from the wise woman's cottage with a bundle of herbs, shrieked like a lapwing when she saw him.

*

I doubt whether Oliver believed in the Royalist cause with anything like the same passion that William showed for Parliament. Oliver was a cavalier because of his loyalty to Sir James, to whom he was grateful for money in his pocket and food in his belly. He was content that things should stay as they were – as they had always been – and not change, considering kings and bishops and parish priests to be part of the natural order of things, without which our world would crumble into dust.

After the Saltley Regiment left Middleholme in January I saw Oliver only once more before the Battle of Marston Moor. It was midsummer. I was rinsing fleeces from our new-shorn sheep on the washing stone outside Top Slack when Oliver rode over the hill from Blackwater Clough. Had it not been for recognizing his horse I might not have known him – so filthy and bedraggled was he and his clothing so tattered and torn. As he got nearer I could see that he was hurt. He was holding the reins with just one hand and the tunic sleeve of his other arm – hanging limply beside his saddle – was soaked red.

'Mother!' I shouted, and she broke off from stirring a pudding and came outside into the sunshine. Father appeared in the doorway, squinting into the light.

'Who is it?' he said, unable to decipher detail from the shadows.

'It is our son,' Mother said.

'William?' Father asked.

'No, sir,' my brother replied. 'Oliver.'

Oliver reached the door and all but fell from his horse. Mother took his arm and led him inside.

'Tether his horse, Abigail,' she said. 'And fetch a bucket of water from the well.'

By the time I entered the house again Mother had peeled back the sticky cloth from Oliver's shoulder and was swabbing at the blood with a torn rag. She dipped the rag into the pail and I saw the water cloud crimson. I remembered what Old Tristram had said – 'Blood will flow like a river' – and I shivered at the memory.

'Bring him food,' Mother said. 'He looks half famished.' I found some ale and bread and set them on the floor beside his feet. Then Oliver, like a boy again in the presence of his mother's nursing, began speaking in a torrent of words. There had been a skirmish just this side of Skipton, he and a dozen of his fellow soldiers ambushed by a division of rebel cavalry. Several of the Saltley men had been killed and the others scattered, pursued across the moors as far as Keighley.

Oliver ate as he talked, cramming handfuls of bread into his mouth as though he had not eaten for days.

'York is under siege,' he said. 'There is no food and some of the soldiers are starving. If York falls they say the King's cause is lost.' The bread was all gone, every last crumb. I brought cheese and a handful of currants, though God knows our own stocks of food were – by then – pitifully low.

Father sat on a stool watching as my mother dabbed at the gash on Oliver's shoulder, packing the gaping wound with a wad of cloth.

'I have seen terrible things, Father,' Oliver said. 'Things I never thought to see. Men mutilated like butchered cattle and women and children driven from their homes by fire.' Oliver winced as my mother pressed against his open flesh. 'And I have done terrible things, too, Father,' he continued. 'Things too terrible for words, that stain my heart . . .'

'Hush now,' my mother said. 'You have done what was asked of you. Nothing more.'

But then my father spoke. 'Change sides, son,' he said. 'Fight for Parliament. Join with William and the others from Lumley Bridge. God is on their side, Oliver. I am certain of it.'

'And be hanged as a turncoat?' Oliver said.

'Hush, Silas,' my mother said. 'Leave the boy. He must do what is right. What his conscience tells him. Let us pray that it will all be finished soon and no one will have to fight for any side.'

*

I was sleeping when William arrived back at Top Slack that night. Raised voices woke me. They were the voices of my brothers on the other side of the curtain, raised not in anger but in fervent debate.

'. . . But at Adwalton Moor your men were a shambles, William,' Oliver was saying. 'They might as well have been girls with pitchforks for all the skills they possessed. Half of them turned tail and ran as soon as the King's armies appeared. I saw cavalrymen kill their own foot soldiers to keep them from fleeing the field . . .'

'But they are better drilled now and ever greater in numbers. They will take York, I am sure of it. Colonel Lambert and Sir Thomas Fairfax and Cromwell . . .'

'Ah yes, the Ironside cavalry, the ones who hear God's voice as they ride into battle . . .'

'Do not mock, brother. These soldiers are men of prayer – clean-living and righteous . . .'

'I never met a soldier yet who didn't drink and womanize whenever he got the chance.'

'The Royalists, Oliver, maybe . . . but these regiments sing psalms together and live according to Scripture.'

'Then they know that to kill a king is against the will of God.'

'We do not plan to kill the King, brother – merely to curb his overweening powers.'

'Powers given him by God almighty.'

'Oliver, I would see not the kingdom of King Charles but the Kingdom of God come on earth.'

'You hope for too much, brother.'

'And you for too little.'

From my bed I could see, through the window, that the dawn was already breaking. I heard the distant clock strike four and tumbled back into sleep.

When I awoke again Oliver was gone.

*

A few days after that William's militia left the valley to march on Wetherby. He took our pony, saying that the army needed every horse they could find to match the force of the King's cavalry. I did not think that Pigeon would be much good in battle as he was lazy and small and slow footed and I was very sad to see him go. I never heard what became of him but he didn't come back to Top Slack.

*

William came back but not before Sam Sowerby had brought us news of a battle on Marston Moor – news which plagued my dreams for many years, so hideous and like Doomsday were his words and the pictures they conjured. Sam spoke of soldiers marching for days at a time, their feet bleeding and their stomachs so empty they could barely stand. Of horses dead in ditches, their bellies gored with pikes. Of dying men trampled underfoot by advancing horses and women following the baggage trains hacked to pieces in the road. Of guns and muskets and colours flying and foot soldiers run through with swords among the hawthorn bushes. Of hailstones and thunder and sodden fields of rye. Of shouts and cannon shots loud enough to wake the dead and the air thick with smoke and the terrible groaning on the field as darkness fell. Of the thousands and thousands dead . . .

*

Sam told us that his brother Henry was dead. That he had seen him fall from his horse on the edge of a bean field and his head sliced from his body by an enemy's sword.

'And . . .' Sam Sowerby said finally. He hesitated as though the words, like a frozen riverbed, were locked fast in his mouth.

'Say it,' my father said. 'Speak the truth.'

I saw Sam's chest rise as he drew in breath.

'Oliver is dead,' he said.

We were standing in the workshop – my parents and I – the loom motionless and silent as if it were holding its breath. When my mother heard this news she ran outside and vomited in the mud. Later, when Sam Sowerby had gone, I heard her in the barn, wailing and drumming her head against the wooden beams. My brother Oliver was just eighteen years old.

Grace

'Sir, I must advise you to leave – it isn't safe for you here!'

Sir James Hallam's steward is at the door. His head is covered with a grey hood, more for disguise than for warmth, since the day is sticky with heat. He speaks to Father in a hushed whisper but his voice travels up the stairs to where I sit, my face pressed against the cool polished rail. Martha leans against my knees, twiddling the fabric of her dress between her nervous fingers.

'Why isn't it safe?' she whispers. Her temples are beaded with sweat. I stroke a damp lock of hair and say, 'Soldiers are coming.'

I do not tell her, though I have overheard – earlier today – Thomas Sunderland telling Father about a priest near Wetherby, murdered in his bed and his body hung from a flagpole in the street as a public spectacle.

'Cromwell's soldiers, bolder with victory, will stop at nothing to wipe out every last trace of popish practice,' I heard Thomas Sunderland say.

'They are killing priests to make an example of them,' Father replies. 'And they believe that God is on their side – that they are like Elijah slaying the Prophets of Baal.'

I remember the story of Elijah – how he railed against the wicked King Ahab and his treacherous wife, Jezebel, and called God to send down fire on to his altar. I think of King Charles and his French wife Henrietta Maria, whom I imagine in lace and pearls with dark eyes like two deep moorland pools. I do not think she is treacherous or that the King is wicked. I have seen a picture of the King and I think he looks kind. His face is sad, though, despite its slender elegance. I think that the King is sad because his people fight and do not love one another.

'Soldiers are coming,' I say again to Martha, smoothing her hair.

'Will they sleep in our beds?' she asks, turning her face upwards towards mine like a flower greeting the sun.

'Perhaps,' I say.

I know from Thomas Sunderland's reports that there has been a battle somewhere called Marston Moor and that many of Sir James's regiment are dead. (At this, standing in my father's study with a book in my hand, I think of Oliver Booth with his handsome face and his strong arms lifting me from his horse and I hope that he is living and will return again to Middleholme.) Father says Parliament's triumphant armies are marching west again, coming over the Pennines, occupying the woollen towns as they go.

'Cromwell's men are only a day's march away, sir,' says the steward at the door, his grey hood slipping on to his shoulders. 'You must get away from here. Quickly!'

Father leaves that night, under cover of darkness. Lady Hallam sends the bay mare, Hazel, for him since – the Scottish soldiers having taken Falcon – Father has no horse of his own to ride on. Hazel's hooves are bound with sacking to muffle their sound on the cobbled lane. Mother presses a loaf of rye bread and a hunk of cheese wrapped in linen into Father's hands and he stows them in the leather bag beside his saddle. Then I see him take a pistol from the saddlebag and slip it into my mother's pocket.

'I fear your need of this will be greater than mine,' he says. I have never seen my father with a weapon before and assume that Lady Hallam has sent it from Saltley for his protection. I wonder what the world has come to when a priest must shoot to save himself.

My mother is weeping now. She clasps Father to her, her rounded belly – now swollen like a peapod – filling the space between the two of them. My father kisses the top of her head as she sobs into his shirt and then, suddenly, he kisses her roughly on the mouth in a way that reminds me of the soldiers with their onion breath. I look away, too embarrassed to embrace him myself, and then he is gone, slipping off into the inky night.

*

Father leaves Middleholme not a moment too soon because the following night I awake to the sound of a hundred troops clattering into the town. Down the hill they come, over the packhorse way past Top Slack, all marching feet and thunder of hooves and laughter and singing. I creep from my bed and peep out of the window, my heart thumping noisily in my chest. Soldiers with flaming clubs are streaming towards the church. I hear the tinkle of smashed glass and the thump of a door kicked down and then, within minutes, tongues of fire are leaping from the roof of the church. I open my bedroom door, hearing it creak like cloth tearing. On the stairs below, my mother is lighting a candle – her skirt pulled on hastily over her night clothes, and her hair tumbling loosely behind her. Tabitha appears in the parlour doorway. She has a knife in her hand, the one she uses for slicing ham from the bone. I see its blade glint in the moonlight that spills from the window. None of us speaks, so filled with fear are we at the sounds of whooping and chanting coming from the street, growing louder with each breath I take. I hold my breath in the hope that they will pass over our house just as the angel of death passed over the houses of the Israelites when Moses led them out of Egypt. But my hope is in vain.

Suddenly there is a terrible bang on the door – a sound like a clap of thunder, a blow of metal against wood.

'Open up!' someone roars. Then a fearful hammering begins, drumming at the door as though they might batter it to pieces.

'Open the door!' they shout again. Mother hides herself under the stairs and Tabitha waits, pressed against the wall, her knife clutched to her chest. Margaret, freshly woken from sleep, comes to my side now and presses her warm body against me, seeking protection.

112

'What's happening?' she says. I take her hand and grip it tightly as if she might slip from my grasp and be lost.

The hammering continues and then, before our eyes, the wood begins to split and splinter until the door bursts from its hinges and four men barge across the threshold into our home.

'Where's the priest?' they shout. Their faces are blackened with soot and their heads are covered so that they look – armed with pikes and axes and pitchforks – like hideous devils, their mouths spitting anger.

'Where's the priest?' they yell again.

Tabitha, waving her knife at them, screams, 'He isn't here!' Tabitha's blade, for all its sharpness, provokes no fear whatsoever in the devils and one of them, pushing her roughly out of the way as he enters the passageway, laughs at her sarcastically.

'Cut me to pieces would you, darling?' he says, giving her a shove.

Now another of the devils sees my mother under the stairs and, seizing her by the wrist, pulls her out of her hiding place.

'Mistress Fowler,' he says. 'The wife of the Papist!' I wonder how he recognizes my mother. Whether, under his sooty disguise, he is someone known to me – some neighbour. He grabs Mother and holds a scythe to her throat. 'Where is he?' he says, menacingly.

'He isn't here!' I shout from the stairs. At the sound of my voice two of the men run up the stairs and push past us into the bedroom. Martha, my sister, cowers beside the window. Ellen, the baby, still sleeping until this moment, wakes up at the sound of rough boots on floorboards and begins to scream. I run to her and try to snatch her from the bed but the soldier, pitchfork in hand, pursues me and, reaching the bed first, grabs Ellen in his filthy arms.

He holds her in front of him like a bundle of corn, her terrified legs thrashing as she screams.

'Tell me where you've hidden the priest, or I'll kill the child,' he says.

'He isn't here,' I say urgently. 'He's gone. For the love of God in heaven, sir, spare my sister! My father is gone and we do not know where ...'

Now the other devil who came upstairs begins to search the room. He overturns the bedstead and spills linen from a chest. He tugs a curtain so violently that it tears from its rail and tumbles to the floor. Unable to find any trace of my father he smashes a pitcher on the floor and hurls a candlestick at the wall. Then he takes a knife from his belt and slashes the bolster so that feathers fly all over the room in an angry flurry. Downstairs I can hear more smashing and rummaging – the slam of doors and the thump of drawers pulled too roughly from their sockets. The breaking of pots and the clatter of pewter plates on stone.

'He isn't here!' I hear Tabitha scream but still the devils search. Satisfied now that my father isn't concealed under the bedclothes, and wearied of holding a screaming child, the devil with the pitchfork lets go of Ellen and she falls to the floor in a wailing heap. Seizing a pair of Father's boots from the closet and waving them delightedly above his head, the devil-soldier crashes back down the stairs. I scoop Ellen from the floor and set her down beside Margaret and Martha, who cling to her as though they will never let her go.

All four soldiers now rampage through the parlour, breaking everything in their tracks. They upset every pan and jar, kick over every stick of furniture, tear every cloth with their sharp weapons and finally – horror of horrors – one of them (the one with the axe) drops his trousers and defecates in the middle of the floor, like a dog.

'Please, stop!' I yell, unable to stand any more. Tabitha is at my mother's side holding her by the arm lest she faint and my sisters, at the top of the stairs, are screaming until I fear their lungs will burst. The men stop their destruction momentarily, amused by my boldness.

'Please, stop,' I say. 'My mother is about to have a child.'

'And would you like one, too, darling?' one of them says and he grabs me and presses himself against me in a vile way.

'LEAVE HER!' My mother's voice rings out across the room. When I look round I see that she is standing upright, holding a cocked pistol, and pointing it at the soldier's back.

'Leave the girl and leave this house!' she shouts and, with a flourish, she fires the pistol at the wall. I look at her in amazement and then, to my great astonishment, the four men turn and leave the house – laughing uproariously and taking with them as much of our copper and linen and plate as their foul arms can carry.

*

So shocked is my poor mother by the soldiers' intrusion and by her own valiant response that, within the hour, she falls into the throes of childbirth.

'It is too soon,' Tabitha says, searching for a pail in the chaos of overturned things in the parlour. 'The bairn will be too small. It isn't her time yet.' My mother is groaning, bent double over an upturned table, one hand clutching at her belly, the other gripping a spoon so tightly her knuckles flash white.

*

I go to fetch the midwife, hurrying across Market Bridge as the dawn begins to break, gripped with terror at the sight of houses burning and women being pulled from their homes by their hair. But the midwife will not come. She says she is too afraid to leave her cottage when the streets are full of soldiers and so I run home again, muttering prayers under my breath as I go.

'She won't come,' I say, bursting into the parlour.

'There is no need,' Tabitha says quietly.

The baby is born already and he is dead. He is no bigger than a kitten and lies, in the bottom of the pail, pink and slippery as a skinned rabbit.

Abigail

The fires were still burning by morning following the night the Roundhead soldiers returned to Middleholme. From Top Slack we could see tongues of flame rising from the valley like dancing flags.

William came home that morning with Joseph Crabtree and Isaac Clegg's youngest son, Job. He was unharmed – all except for a cut on his forehead that looked like a stray lock of hair. His regiment had fought well, he said, and unlike most others their casualties had been mercifully few. There seemed little joy in the victory, though. William had a hardness and a deadness about him that chilled my bones. He was like a pond that has frozen over in winter – lifeless and sealed. When my mother told him of Oliver's death he shed no tears.

*

'Nathan Horsfall says the church is all burnt out like a shell,' said my father.

'That will please your Puritan friends,' my mother said sourly. 'Black walls and not a scrap of Roman rags.'

'And Fowler?' Will said, looking through the front window at the pillars of smoke hanging over the town.

'Fled,' my father said. 'Vanished into the air.' This was the first I had heard of the Reverend Fowler's disappearance and I was filled immediately with concern for Grace's safety.

'And Mr Fowler's family?' I asked. 'His wife and daughters? Are they fled, too?'

'Your Papist friends?' Will said, scowling through the glass. I did not respond.

'The vicarage is empty, so Nathan Horsfall says – ransacked in the night.'

'And are they dead?' my mother asked.

'Dead or gone. Either way – good riddance to them!' William said. I saw the faintest trace of a smile flicker across his mouth and hated him for it.

*

Later, sitting down to eat, Father gave his Bible to William and asked him to read a psalm for us – since Father's eyes were now too poor to read. William read aloud: 'I will call upon the Lord, who is worthy to be praised: so shall I be saved from mine enemies.'

I could not then – nor can I now – think of our neighbours as enemies. How could Lady Hallam or Henry Sowerby or my brother Oliver be an enemy to me?

Father pushed his chair back from the table and pinched the brow of his nose. He said that he hoped Cromwell and his men would restore good Protestant ways in England and that the King – chastened by his failure on the battle-field – would now surrender to his Parliament and rule in a just and godly way.

'Then we shall eat again and weave our cloth and live in peace,' he said, licking his fingers and gathering up the last few precious crumbs of bread from his plate.

'And Oliver will not have died to no purpose,' my mother added.

*

I could not eat – hungry as I was – for worrying about Grace. Where would I look for her if she was gone? How would I find her again if she was fled from her home? The only place I could think to look was on the Hill of the Angels and so, slipping from our house as soon as I could escape my brother's notice, I made my way hastily towards the crags. I might have taken more care but fear made me reckless. The sun was bright and hot and I began to sweat from the effort of the climb. On the sloping side of the moor the bilberry bushes were laden with fat black fruit. I paused for a moment to catch my breath and picked a few – staining my fingers purple. Their sour juices made my eyes smart but I crammed them into my mouth nonetheless.

When I reached the Winstone Rocks I wriggled through the gap in the stones and saw straight away, and with a surge of joy, that the angels were there – dancing on the cave wall.

'Grace,' I called, hopeful of finding my friend there, too. No one answered but I sensed with sudden concern that I wasn't alone in the cave. As my eyes adjusted to the gloom I could see there was a bundle of something on the floor – what looked like a pile of rags, heaped on top of the bracken.

119

'Grace,' I said again, stepping forward. There was a strong smell – a dungy, ripe unwashed smell. Not Grace Fowler's smell. More the scent of a man.

The bundle of cloth moved a little and I saw it was a person, lying on its side, back towards me.

'Grace?' I said a third time, my heart pounding in my chest.

'Who's there?' the person said. It was a man's voice – and a frightened one at that. As he lifted his head I saw a flash of red hair.

'Show yourself,' I said boldly, and the man rolled over until he was facing me.

Immediately I recognized him. It was the stonemason's boy – the one Grace and I had watched years earlier, helping Joseph the stonemason carve Thomas Sunderland's angel. The one who had mended the bridge when the flood brought it down. He looked at me with wide terrified eyes.

'Don't tell Cromwell's men I'm here,' he said fearfully, 'or they'll hang me.'

'Why? Are you for the King?' I asked.

'No, for Parliament,' he said, propping himself up on his elbows.

'Then why would they hang you?' I asked. 'Middleholme is a Roundhead town again.'

'Because I'm a deserter,' he said, and it was then that I saw that the bracken he was lying on was stained scarlet with his blood.

Grace

Snip. The cold blade of the scissors brushes against my neck as my hair falls in clumps on to the stone floor. In front of me, Margaret holds up a looking glass no bigger than my hand. I sit on an upturned pail, stretching out lengths of my hair, horizontally, with my left hand and chopping off chunks of it with the shears in my right. The room is dark, for it has only one small window, but I can see the gleam of my younger sister's eyes as they watch me in horrified wonder. Martha bends down and picks up a lock of my hair and presses it to her cheek. Ellen, standing beside me, reaches up her chubby hand to stroke the shorn tufts that stand up from my scalp now, like a field of stubble after the corn is harvested. Only the length at the back remains now and I lift my elbows to reach it with the scissors so that my shadow on the wall looks like some strange winged beast. *Snip*. The shears close their sharp mouth over my hair and it falls to the ground without a sound.

Margaret gathers the strands into a bundle which she ties with a length of twine. The bundle is thicker than a horse's

121

tail and almost as long. She sets it on the table reverently, as though it were a dead creature.

'Quick, before Mother wakes,' I say. 'Or she will weep yet more.'

I take off my ragged dress and pull from a sack the clothes the blacksmith's wife gave us the night we hid in the forge – the night after my mother's baby was born dead. They are boys' clothes – rough breeches and a coarse shirt and a cap to hide what is left of my hair. Once I am dressed Margaret holds the mirror for me again.

'There,' I say. 'I am your brother now. Don't call me Grace. Call me Jack.'

'Jack Fowler,' says Martha, and then she giggles.

*

After the soldiers searched our house, the night the church was set on fire, Tabitha said it wasn't safe for us to stay at the vicarage. She said the soldiers would come back and take more than our bed sheets and our plates. She said they would harm us – knowing us to be alone, and believing us to be – like my father – traitors to Cromwell's cause. She took us to the house of Nathan Horsfall, the black-smith, down beside the river. He is loyal to the King and to Sir James and his wife is a kind and gentle woman. She gave us food and hid us in the forge, in a room that became so hot that we might have been in hell. My mother could do nothing but sob, so distressed was she by all that had happened. She rocked herself like a child and tugged so hard on her hair that it parted from her scalp in handfuls.

122

On our third day there I dressed in Jack Horsfall's clothes and made my way to Saltley Hall, believing that calling upon the charity of Lady Hallam was our best hope now that Father was gone. The journey to Saltley Hall was fraught with danger, despite my boy's appearance. The hillside above the town was dotted with soldiers and I had to hide or lie low in the grass several times before I reached the Hallams' estate. Darting my way through the gate I crept towards the house, keeping to the edge of the wood for cover.

I found Lady Hallam quite well, though she is a prisoner in her own house now that Saltley is overrun with enemy troops. She still has her maid and one of her cooks but the house is so raided and plundered that I could scarcely recognize the room we sat in. Only the green chairs remained and they were all stripped of their cushions and braid. The house was quite bare. I wonder that Roundhead soldiers have any use for fine curtains and delicate glass. They cannot be worth much now with the fashion for plainness everywhere around. I think they take them away out of spite for it seems the Puritans would have all finery destroyed.

*

Lady Hallam spoke only briefly to me as she said she feared for my safety despite my disguise. She said there was news that Father had reached Skipton and was within the castle with those of Sir James's troops who had survived Marston Moor. She said that there was an empty cottage on the estate, down beside the Lumley, close to the West Bridge, that we could live in till the trouble had passed.

'I have no pony to give you for the soldiers have taken every last one and there is no money for food so you will have to fend for yourselves but at least you will have a roof over your heads. I suggest you keep your boys' clothes. You will be the safer for them.' She kissed me and as we said goodbye she had such a weight of sadness in her face that I wanted to weep, as my mother weeps.

*

I take the bundle of hair which is wrapped now in a piece of rag and close the cottage door quietly behind me. Mother is still sleeping, which is a blessing to us all. Only when she sleeps is she at peace and free from the fretting that seems to grow worse each day. Margaret waves to me from the window. I fear for my sisters' safety leaving them unattended but I know I must find work or we will all starve. Tabitha has left us since we moved to the cottage by the river. Her mother is sick and since her father was killed in a skirmish on Rochdale Moor there is no one to care for her brothers and sisters so she is returned home to her family. We miss her pies and her warm-hearted chatter.

*

I make my way east along the riverbank towards the town. Looking north up the narrow wooded cleft of Coldwater Dene I can just make out the Winstone Rocks on the hill above the trees. I think of the angels and our tiny store of treasures. My peacock feather and Abigail's eggshell and the pearly button and the hank of wool. I think of the face of Jesus spilled on the floor of the cave like rain.

124

I have not seen Abigail Booth since the day her brother William called me a witch. Barely half a year has passed but our visits to the Hill of the Angels seem, already, like something from another life. Since then, soldiers have gone and more soldiers have come, Father has fled, Mother has given birth to a dead child and all but lost her wits, and we are poor as beggars. And I am Jack, in boys' clothes.

'Papist witch!' I hear William's words again and see his hate-filled face and the pleasure with which he dashed the coloured glass on to the rock. How can two brothers be so different? When I think of Oliver Booth I picture him smiling and with clouds of angels dancing round his head.

I wonder if Abigail still visits the cave and if she thinks me a witch, too. I wonder if *she* now thinks that beauty is to be feared. That those who treasure things somehow displease God? Has William tainted her – the way a rotten egg will spoil the taste of good eggs – so that she hates me, too? Calls me Papist? Believes me to be traitorous? Or has she forgotten me?

The July sun is hot and the ground beneath my unshod feet is all shrunk to dust. Beside the path, willowherb blazes royal purple and at its colour I feel my mood brighten. Surely the King will soon defeat the parliamentarian rebels and order and beauty will come again to our land. Father will come back to Middleholme and celebrate Mass in a cope more lovely than the one they burned – a white one, as bright as new-fallen snow. And Mother will be well again.

*

I stay beside the river as far as Market Bridge in order to bypass the town, using the path that keeps to the riverbank. In places the river has dried almost to a trickle and I sit, briefly, with my feet in the shallows, feeling the water sluice over my ankles. Someone is driving a group of scraggly sheep over the bridge so I wait down below until the coast is clear and then I cross the river quickly and head up the lane beside Middleholme church. Foolish as it is, I cannot stop myself entering the churchyard and peering in at the south door, which stands wide open. The church, with its patched roof, is a barracks now – home to a hundred or more soldiers and stable to their horses. I can see piles of dung and heaps of straw where once we knelt in prayer and I am glad Father cannot see the filth and foulness that are there. A soldier comes from the door, with his arms around a woman. She is laughing and her blouse is all unbuttoned.

'Keep your eyes to yourself, young 'un,' she says as she passes me and I pull my hat down further over my eyes to hide my face.

'You've made the lad blush,' the soldier says, slapping her across the rump as though she were a horse.

I pass the vicarage, thinking of all the things we left behind – Mother's dresses bundled in the closet and Father's books and the cradle where Ellen slept and all the fine bed linen my mother had stitched. When we went by night to Nathan Horsfall's house we took only what we could carry – a pewter jug, a basin, a few plates, a hog's hair brush, a tiny looking glass, a carving knife and the pistol with which my mother defended us the night after Father left Middleholme. There are signs that soldiers are there now and I wonder what harm they have done to our things and what brutality and vileness our walls have been witness to.

Crossing the lane, I turn into the garden of Thomas Sunderland's house and, standing beneath the comforting gaze of the angel over his door, I strike the bell.

'May I speak with your master?' I say when a serving girl answers.

'He isn't home,' she says. She looks at me suspiciously and I drop my eyes to the floor in case she recognizes my face.

'I'm happy to wait,' I reply.

'You'd better come through here,' she says and she leads me into the parlour. There, to my amazement, I see the font cover – the one my father rescued in the dead of night – hanging from a ceiling beam, completely unharmed. I let out a gasp which causes her to look suspiciously at me again.

'Wait here,' she says. When she leaves me I go immediately to the wooden cover, rising to the rafters like a steeple, and place my arms around it as if I were embracing a lost friend. The wood feels cool against my skin and smells of candlewax. I run my fingers over the carved scenes, reading their familiar stories.

'How can I help you?' Master Sunderland says suddenly and I turn round, startled and foolish, and fall to my knees in front of him.

'God bless you, sir,' I say.

I tell him my mother is sick and my father gone away with the war and that my sisters and I need work carding and spinning wool and that I know him to be merciful and a man of God.

'And can you card and spin?' he says.

'No, sir, but I learn fast,' I say. 'I promise, sir, I will work hard for you.'

I glance up and see that he is looking at my hands.

'Have you a spindle and cards?' he says. As he asks his question a grey dog trots in through the open door. It is Boy. I have played with him often in the lane beside our house. He comes to me, still kneeling on the floor, and licks my face with a great swish of his hairy tail which makes his master laugh.

'I have not, sir,' I say.

'Come, Boy,' Master Sunderland says, calling the dog to his side. 'I shall provide you with them.'

'We have no money to pay you,' I say. 'But I have this.' I pull the bundle of hair from my pocket and unwrap it for him to see. He takes it from me and holds it up to the light streaming in at the window.

'This will fetch a fair price from a wigmaker in London,' he says. He is staring at me, running his eyes over my clothes, my face, my stature.

'It is my sister's,' I say.

'If you wish it, I will have my son trade it for you when he is next in the City and see that you are paid. There is no charge for the spinning wheel since you will be my employee.'

'Thank you, sir,' I say. 'You are most generous.'

'Come tomorrow morning to my workshop and you will be shown your trade. I shall see that tools and a bundle of fleeces are delivered to your cottage by the end of the week. Where is it that you live, boy?'

'On the Saltley Estate, sir,' I say, 'by the West Bridge. The last cottage in the row, sir.'

'And what is your name?'

'Jack, sir,' I say, feeling my face smart. Thomas Sunderland is looking closely at me. I meet his eye and he smiles. I know in that moment that he has recognized me – that he knows exactly who I am – and I brace myself for his anger. But he goes on smiling.

'Jack what?' he says. I hesitate, and then I say, 'Jack Fowler, sir,' and he nods.

'I pray your father is well, Jack,' he says. 'Goodbye.'

As I leave Thomas Sunderland's house I feel sure the stone angel is smiling at me and I whisper a prayer of thanks to God for his goodness and protection.

Abigail

'Abigail!' I could hear my father calling my name. 'Abigail!' his shout came again. I was hiding behind the well, a pitcher of ale in my hand, a bundle of rags and a stolen chunk of bread tucked in the pockets of my skirt. Glancing around me to be sure that I was unseen, I ran as fast as I could on to the causey path and up the hill towards Blackmoor Top.

The stonemason's apprentice had been shot in the leg with a musket. There was a gaping hole in his thigh and he had lost more blood than a pig at killing time. He was too weak and too frightened to leave the cave, besides which he couldn't stand, let alone walk anywhere. How he came to have reached the Hill of the Angels alone I never knew. I was certain that he had been brought there supernaturally and that the angels were protecting him from further harm. And so, later on the day I found him I stole beer and bread from Top Slack and went back to the Winstone Rocks.

'You didn't tell no one I was here, did you?' he said as I squeezed myself through the gap in the rocks.

'No one,' I said. He gulped the ale down gratefully. When he had drunk it all I took the empty jug to the stream at

Coldwater Clough and filled it with peaty water. Then I went back to the cave to bathe his leg, trying to remember all I had seen my mother do to Oliver's shoulder. As I swabbed with my wet rags, the red-haired boy bit his lip and grimaced with the pain of my touch. The blood had fused his breeches to the skin and as I prised them free from the ragged flesh I felt him flinch so violently I stopped what I was doing. But he urged me to continue.

'Just do it – and quickly,' he said, clenching his teeth.

I packed the musket wound with moss – wet and springy from the moor – and bound it tightly with strips of rag to stop the bleeding. As I worked, the angels danced brightly on the rock wall and I felt myself blessed. When I'd finished I brought more bracken into the cave to make him comfortable and then I washed his blood-soaked clothes in the stream – drying them in the afternoon sun.

*

For two weeks and more I visited the stonemason's boy in the cave at the Winstone Rocks, saving portions of my own food where I could and taking a crust of bread here, a lump of cheese there, in the hope that no one would notice my theft. I could never stay for long as it was harvest time and there was already too much to do at Top Slack but he always appeared glad to see me. For the first few days he seemed to suffer greatly. Once he was delirious with a fever, crying out in pain, like a yelping fox. I found a piece of dried stick for him to bite on and picked sprigs of thyme from among

131

the rocks to try to ease his pain. But little by little he began to grow stronger.

At first we were shy with each other and spoke very little. He expressed his thanks for my care of him.

'Thank you, Miss . . . God bless you, Miss . . . You are an angel to me, Miss.'

The boy was worried he'd be found and made a spectacle of. There were rumours of deserters who'd been hanged from trees by their necks and of rewards paid to those who turned them in. I assured him over and over of his safety.

'No one knows you are here,' I said. 'The cave is quite secret.'

But I was afraid it was not. I was conspicuous, climbing each day up the crags with provisions in my hands. There were no trees to hide me, no woods to serve as cover on the blasted, treeless moor. And there were soldiers on the hill, bands of men and scouts on horses watching over the town, waiting for the King's soldiers to strike again.

Then, one morning, my mother put a fresh baked loaf into my hands and said, quietly, 'Is it Miss Fowler you are hiding?' I did not answer but I knew my mother had read my face and nothing was hidden from her.

'Is it the priest?' I shook my head.

'Who, then?' my mother whispered.

'I cannot say,' I murmured.

'Be careful, Abigail,' she said. I was still holding the warm bread which felt so comforting in my hands that I wanted to kiss it and my mother, too.

*

'Quick, hide it, before William sees,' my mother said, handing me a piece of sackcloth.

*

I took the loaf to the stonemason's boy and found him sitting up, drawing with a chalky pebble on the wall of the cave. He was drawing angels – delicate winged creatures with kind faces and soft hair. When I saw them something deep inside me seemed to dance.

'I do not know your name,' I said.

'Samuel,' he replied.

'Do you think you can walk, Samuel?' I asked. 'I think we should move you somewhere lower down the valley. Somewhere more secret.'

So I moved my patient at first light – him leaning on my shoulder, dragging his injured leg and walking with a crutch he'd fashioned from a whittled branch. I took him to Clegg's fulling mill, which for more than a year had stood idle and derelict. And there I hid him in a shed, concealed by boxes and buckets and coils of rope.

*

That summer, the summer I was fourteen, my brother William began to talk more and more like a Leveller. He and his friend Hugh Fry from Lumley Bridge – weary of the war and the slowness of its conclusion, frustrated by the promise of soldiers' pay, owed to them but never coming, impatient to bring about the coming of 'The Kingdom' and hungry both for food and for change – began to circulate pamphlets that talked of equality and freedom.

'Read it to me,' my father said as he sat outside Top Slack, tying new-shorn fleeces in a bundle. Our sheep were few that year and their fleeces paltry. Father had learned to do many things by touch so that his failing eyesight was less of a hindrance than it had been at first, but he could no longer see to read, which was a great sadness to him.

William, sitting in the saddle of his new horse – an ugly black thing that flattened its ears and tried to kick at me whenever I came near it – read from the pamphlet in his hand. 'All are by nature equal and alike in power, dignity, authority and majesty. None shall, by nature, have power over another. All who believe on the name of the Lord Jesus shall be called children of God, needing no priests to speak on behalf of them to Almighty God, nor kings to rule over them. In Christ there is neither servant nor master for all are one ...'

'Why, Father,' said Will, pausing to wave the paper above his head so that it flapped like a sail, 'should the likes of Sir James Hallam live in wealth and splendour while you live here, scraping a living with a few measly sheep?'

'I don't think Sir James and Lady Hallam live in much splendour now,' said my mother, who was pegging laundry in the sun. '*He* is nowhere to be seen and they say Saltley is so pillaged and ransacked, and the deer all poached from the woods, that there is nothing left of their wealth ...'

'And rightly so, some might say,' said my father, snapping a length of twine with his teeth. 'Doesn't Scripture promise "He has exalted the poor and sent the rich, hungry away"?'

'It's not Sir James has made us hungry. It's this wretched war,' my mother said, slapping a wet shirt down on a stone. 'We had plenty enough to eat before the fighting began and you were all turned soldiers. And more than a few measly sheep, too, and you wanted for nothing, William Booth!'

'I wanted for justice, Mother, and for change and for a land where God is feared and people are free.'

I watched William fold the pamphlet inside his soldier's tunic and ride towards Middleholme. Then I took the bundle of fleeces from Father and stowed them in the workshop.

*

Since the Battle of Marston Moor, the Fowlers seemed to have disappeared completely. I missed Grace very much and thought of her often. A new vicar had come in her father's place – a Puritan called Eli Braithwaite. He had no family and seemed content to share his house with a dozen soldiers. He wore no ribbons in his hair and was as plain as sackcloth and he preached angry sermons about hell and the devil. Where the stained glass windows had been, behind the pulpit, were now boards – blank and drear – and try as I might to fix my eyes on Jesus I felt only a heaviness in my heart as I knelt to pray there.

*

It seemed Middleholme had become a husk of what it once was – ragged and weary and sad. Looking down at the streets of the town and the squat black church and the river snaking along the valley bottom I struggled to remember what the town had been like before war began. It was a windy day in August. I was sitting outside on a stool, carding wool, brushing the fleecy fibres backwards and forwards on the wiry teeth of the comb, when my brother came into view on his ugly black horse. He was riding at some speed towards Top Slack, eastwards across the fell from Blackwater Clough. Father was in the workshop and Mother was finishing a kersey, cropping shears in hand.

'Here's Will,' I shouted. But no sooner had I stood up and set my cards on the step when Will flung himself from his horse and grabbed me by the hair. Tugging roughly at my scalp he dragged me inside the house and thrust me into the workshop.

'This girl,' he roared. 'Not content with witchcraft and idol worship' – he pushed me so hard that I struck my head against the corner of the loom – 'is now harbouring deserters! Cowards who leave the field of battle like rats running from a sinking ship!'

I stood up again, rubbing my head and finding a smear of blood on the palm of my hand.

'What are you talking about? What does he mean, Abigail?' my father said, furrowing his brow. I did not answer.

William shoved me again with his fist.

'You were seen,' he said. 'Job Clegg spotted you. Taking good food to a filthy traitor! May you rot in hell, sister.'

'What have you done to him?' I said.

'You don't deny it, then?' William answered, glowering at me.

136

'Where is he?' I said, panic rising in my throat.

'Job Clegg has him. And will hand him over to his commanders, who will most likely chop off his head and stick it on a pike ...'

'No,' I yelled, running at my brother and pounding his chest with my fists.

'What's he to you?' William said, mockingly, catching me by the wrists.

'A friend,' I said. 'One who fears God and is as much a child of His as you and I are, William ...'

'He had better fear Cromwell, too, and know that a soldier's place is to stand and fight.' William spat his words into my face. 'Not run away like a girl ...'

'Let her go, William Booth,' said my mother behind me. 'Abigail works harder round here than you do and I'll not have her slighted so ...'

'And I'll not take orders from a woman,' William said, staring at our mother and gripping my wrists more tightly.

'No, but you'll take them from me!' boomed my father's voice as he rose from his stool, drawing himself up to his full height. I had rarely heard him shout so loud.

'Let Abigail go and tell me, in God's name, who you're talking about!'

William freed my arms and I fell to the floor before my father's feet.

'Father, be merciful,' I said.

I told him that Samuel the stonemason's apprentice had come to the Winstone Rocks with grave injuries, that

137

he had witnessed nameless horrors at Marston Moor, that God had sent him to me and that I had cared for him in mercy and in kindness, and that he was now at Clegg's mill, hiding.

'Hiding no more, lass,' William said, 'now that Job Clegg has smelt him out!'

'Job Clegg is a greedy fool,' my mother said, 'hungry for blood payment, I'll not doubt.'

'Let him come here, Father,' I said. 'He will be strong again soon. He can work for his keep. We can hide him. No one will know who he is . . .'

'All the town will know,' exclaimed William. 'He has a head of hair the colour of rowan berries.'

'He can cut his hair and smear his beard with soot,' I said. 'We can say he is my uncle's son, come from Todmorden to help us with our kerseys.' I was on my knees before my father.

'He is a deserter, sister!' William said, dismayed at my request to harbour him.

It was then that I remembered the Scriptures that say, 'Come, ye blessed of my Father, inherit the kingdom, for I was hungry and ye gave me meat: I was thirsty and ye gave me drink: I was a stranger, and ye took me in,' and I uttered them aloud, feeling, as I spoke, that God had put the words into my mouth. Mother was watching me, holding my gaze, then, pressing her finger to her lips, she stepped from the workshop into the passageway. My father sighed deeply. 'Does the Lord not say, "I desire mercy, not sacrifice"?' he said. I was still kneeling at his feet. Seizing the tops of his boots I said, 'Please, Father.'

Father turned to face my brother and said, 'William, go to Clegg's mill and bring the stonemason's boy—'

'But Job Clegg . . .' my brother interrupted him.

'Tell Job Clegg,' said Father, raising his voice, 'he should listen to Old Tristram. Does he not say, "Only the merciful shall be saved"? Go, fetch the boy!'

'I will take no such orders,' said William defiantly. 'I am a soldier in the armies of Parliament . . .'

'And I am *your father*!' my father roared. 'And Scripture says, "Honour thy father and thy mother"!'

William adjusted the buckle on his belt. 'Even if I keep your secret, Job Clegg will never stay silent. He is his father's son.'

'Then give him this,' said Mother, striding past the loom to place a bag of coins in William's hand.

'What's this?' my brother asked.

'Three pounds, fifteen shillings and sixpence – more than Mr Cromwell will pay him!' Mother wiped her hands on her apron and fixed William with a birdlike stare. Father was looking at her in amazement. 'Hannah?' he said, gesturing to the bundle of coins in William's hands.

'Nineteen years I've been saving this, penny by penny, groat by groat – and every coin has the King's head on it!'

I'd seen my mother once, late, when she thought us all sleeping, slide the linen chest aside and lift the loose stone flag. I'd seen the pudding cloth tied with string and heard the chink of coins, hard saved. And now she would give it all to have Samuel spared.

William shook his head. 'And you'd waste it all on this coward,' he said quietly. 'If you bring this traitor into our house, I will never come here again.'

'Then that will be your choice, William,' my father replied.

*

So it was, that on an August night when the harvest moon was high in the sky, in the year that I was fourteen, Samuel the stonemason's boy came to live at Top Slack and William, clutching my mother's bag of treasure, rode off on his ugly black horse.

Grace

'Listen!' Margaret says. She is helping me wrap the skeins of woollen yarn we have spun. I stand still to listen. 'Ssh! There it is again,' she says, cocking her head on one side like a bird and keeping still as stone.

It has been snowing heavily in the night and the cottage is very cold. I have made a small fire which burns feebly in the grate. Mother sits by it stitching, though the light – with snow piled high on the window ledge – is so gloomy and poor I wonder she can see her needle.

'Can't you hear it, Grace?' Margaret says, and I walk to the door, pressing my ear up against the damp timber.

'Miaow!' There is a thin mewing sound, high-pitched and insistent.

'Yes,' I say. 'I can hear it, too.'

'Open the door.' Margaret pushes past me and lifts the latch. The weight of snow against the door has wedged it shut and we have to lean with all our weight to make it budge, but as soon as it is a few inches ajar a tiny black kitten shoots in, skimming past our legs.

'Look!' my sister cries, smiling with delight, and Martha and Ellen, playing together in the corner, creep from the shadows full of curiosity.

The kitten has particles of snow on his whiskers and ears and snow sticks to his paws as though he is wearing white stockings. As soon as he is inside the cottage he shakes himself so that the flakes fall from him, leaving him midnight black. Then he heads purposefully for the fire and begins to thread himself in and out of Mother's legs, purring so loudly he seems to make the whole house vibrate.

I leave my sisters squealing with pleasure at our furry visitor and, taking the parcel of wool, shove my way out of the snow-blocked door. Outside the cottage, the drifts are so deep they come over my boots. The snow has stopped falling now and the sun is shining so brightly that my eyes take a moment to adjust to the glare. Stepping from the smoky gloom of our house into this dazzling white world I could believe that I had entered paradise and that Middleholme had somehow been transformed into the Heavenly City. I wish it were so and that Father, robed in white and gold, would walk towards me along the banks of the icy stream. These imaginings warm me as I walk eastwards towards the town and for a moment I forget my aching shoulders and the cold and my mother's sadness that seems – sometimes – so deep that we might all drown in it.

I walk to Thomas Sunderland's house, my hat pulled down over my boy's hair, the bundle of wool heavy on my shoulders. The serving girl leads me into the loom shed where my master's younger son, Richard, checks the wool

I have brought, pays me and gives me another sack of uncarded fleece. As I am making my way along the passageway to leave, Master Sunderland – seeing me through an open doorway – calls my name.

'Jack,' he says softly.

'Sir?' I reply.

'Step in here for a moment, boy.' I do as he says and step into the parlour where the font cover hangs silently from the ceiling beams, like a wooden finger pointing skywards.

'I have something for you,' Thomas Sunderland says. Boy, his grey dog, lopes towards me and presses his wet nose against my hand.

'Sir?' I say expectantly.

'My son is newly returned from London. He found a wigmaker much delighted by your sister's hair.' As he says this he stretches out his hand and presses four shiny coins into my hand. I feel the cool weight of them in my palm and looking into Mr Sunderland's kind face I feel so grateful that, were it not unseemly, I would spread myself on the floor and kiss his feet.

'Thank you, sir,' I say.

His face turns grave.

'My son also brought news of the war,' he says. 'Skipton Castle is under siege but there is hope the King's troops will relieve it as they did at Donnington and that reinforcements will come from Ireland. Pray God it may all end soon, Jack.'

I nod. And then I say, 'Is it true that Archbishop Laud is dead?' I have heard murmurings in the market place.

'I fear it is,' he says. 'He was executed in the Tower a week ago.'

*

When I step out into the street again the blue sky has turned milky and the watery sun is wreathed in cloud. Snow is quickly turning to slush and rivulets of meltwater drip from every roof. I see Old Tristram sitting in the lane, huddled over his tin bowl, and wonder if I should give him one of the coins in my pocket since rarely in all of my life have I been so rich. But then I think of my hungry sisters and Martha with no shoes to wear, and Ellen who coughs so much that some nights none of us can sleep from the sound of her, and my mother whose hands are bright red from carding wool and I close my fingers tightly around the coins and hurry past. I see Old Tristram lift his shuttered eyes and say, 'The moon will turn blood red and birds shall fall from the sky and on that day the Lord shall separate the wheat from the chaff.'

*

It is snowing again now – fine sleety snow that whips my face and wets my clothes. I see Sir James's kitchen maid buying onions in the market square and think of Lady Hallam. Then my mind turns to Father. I miss him with an ache in my belly that is bigger than hunger. And yet, though I long for news of him and some promise that he will return, I find to my shame that I cannot quite remember his face – that his image slips from me as vague and insubstantial as fog.

At that moment a horse canters by me and sprays up slush, already oily and grey with the filth of Middleholme's streets. I change my sack of wool from my right shoulder on to my left and wipe the spots of cold dirt from my face with the sleeve of my coat.

At the corner of Corn Street a boy no older than Martha is fastened in the stocks, his hands and feet pinned in front of him and his clothing soaked from sitting in melting snow. Egg yolk runs in trickles down his forehead, congealing like candle wax. I stare at him, wondering what crime one so small can have committed, and smile out of sympathy but he takes my expression for mockery and scowls back at me with an angry face. I feel tears prick at the corners of my eyes and look away. The street is full of soldiers. The town is full of bitterness. Archbishop Laud is dead, his head cut from his body by enemies of the King.

Turning towards the West Bridge I pass a butcher's yard and see, swinging from a hook, a freshly killed pig – its throat cut and its blood dripping darkly on to the snow. And I hear my father's voice – sonorous and low.

'Though your sins be as scarlet, they shall be as white as snow.'

Abigail

Hugh Fry held out a soldier's coat, torn and frayed down the right-hand side.

'The King's forces are defeated,' he said. 'Cromwell has the victory, and God's victory it is – to him be the glory!'

He told us of a battle somewhere called Naseby. 'Ten days' march from here among bean fields and furze bushes and so many rabbit holes you had a job not to lose your foot in one.'

My mother took the coat and folded it on her lap, stroking the red cloth. I imagined William's excitement at joining the New Model Army.

'No more higgledy-piggledy bands of militia. This is a proper army with pay and proper training ... and uniforms!' I heard my brother saying and I pictured him – as he'd been in happier times – twirling proudly in front of us in his scarlet coat and Mother rolling her eyes, telling him he looked like John Sowerby's cockerel.

'He fought fearlessly,' Hugh Fry continued. 'You'd have been proud of him.' None of us could bear to look at him. I could smell fire and mud on his clothes and on the red tunic – and a smell of sweat and fear that made my stomach lurch. Father rested his hand on Mother's shoulder. I could see her body shaking silently.

'After Prince Rupert's cavalry charged on us and the colours fell there was hard fighting among the infantrymen. The pikemen – myself and William included – held back a second cavalry charge. It was raining so hard the field was like a swamp and men were falling on either side of us but William fought on valiantly. Cromwell said the men's bravery made his heart sing praises to God and that the dead would join the saints as surely as Christ is risen.'

'Did you see him die?' my father asked quietly. Hugh Fry bowed his head and said, 'I saw William knock the King's commander off his horse and skewer his thigh with a pike. And then, moments later, William was hit by a musket ball that pierced his armour. I saw him fall but the air was so full of cannon smoke that I never saw nothing more ...'

I did not weep. It was as though my tears had all dried up and my heart was hardened to a crust. Perhaps it was hardened with fury – fury at the memory of my brother's fingers tugging my hair, the slap of his palm, the stab of his words, 'May you rot in hell, sister!' Indignation still seethed and boiled in me.

*

That was in June 1645, the year I was fifteen. We struggled with the harvest that summer. Mother seemed to have grown old overnight and Father was now all but blind. Cromwell was true to his word, though, when it came to paying his

147

troops and we received a small amount of soldier's pay that was still owing to William after his death. With it we bought a new pony – a white pony, whom I named Dandelion, because his mane was like dandelion fluff. But after three long years of civil war we had little and life was harsh. Most of our sheep had been slaughtered or stolen and without my brothers we could no longer manage to weave kerseys. We were thin from lack of food and Mother had a cough that rasped like a rusty wheel. In the autumn of that year, I went to Thomas Sunderland who – God bless his soul – was still prospering from the trade of woollen cloth. (Had it not been for him, I believe all Middleholme might have starved.) I threw myself on his mercy and asked to be employed as a cottager – carding and spinning and finishing cloth. So, in October the year William died, I became the sole supporter of my family.

*

Samuel by then had been at Top Slack for over a year. Gradually his body was healing – and his mind, too, though he spoke little of what he had seen in battle. He still lacked strength and limped badly, so that his body lurched from side to side as he walked, like a cart with a broken wheel. Until the summer William died, Samuel kept hidden, sleeping in the barn, his red hair concealed by a woollen cap. But as time went by and no one came to arrest him, bit by bit he lowered his guard and began to accompany us about our business. Little by little, Samuel became like another son to my parents. He slept where William had

148

once slept and took Oliver's place at table. By the fireside of an evening, he would play upon a pipe he'd fashioned from a whittled stick and Father would sing, moist-eyed. Though Samuel's hair was fiery, his manners were mild and peaceable. Though he did not spin or weave, he was good with his hands and could mend and make things. Trained well by Joseph the stonemason, he was skilled with a hammer and chisel and could chip and carve at lumps of stone, making a face, or a steeple, or a fox, or the letters of a name. Hearing from Mother how it saddened her that she had no grave for William or Oliver – both of whose bodies, I imagined, had rotted in the fields where they fell – Samuel cut a 'W' on one gate pillar and an 'O' on the other, that our farm gate might serve as a memorial to my two dead brothers.

'I am the gate for the sheep,' Father said, tracing the letters with his fingertips.

Though Samuel had not William's sharpness with words, nor Oliver's merry spirit, he was kind and we grew to love him. I was glad of his company and grateful for the warmth he brought to Top Slack.

The spring after William died, Thomas Sunderland bought Clegg's fulling mill and set about restoring it to working order. By summer, when he decided to add to the buildings and install a second water mill, Samuel – by then much recovered – found employment cutting and carving the stone.

*

So things continued much like this for two years or more. On Sundays we walked to church and chanted psalms and

149

listened to the rantings of Eli Braithwaite – which were less well-received than they once had been. Every week I took Dandelion to Master Sunderland's house and collected wool from the wool drovers. I carded it and spun it and then I took it back to his loom sheds – which were now growing as large as the parish church. Then I fetched shrunk cloth from Coldwater mill and finished it with the cropping shears, folding it in sheets of paper and pressing it flat. Father worked as much as he was able, making rope and leather straps which I sold at market to buy eggs and cheese. Mother kept house and fed us as best she could, and Samuel fashioned stone. His master, Joseph the stonemason, had died at Marston Moor, so Samuel's skills were much needed in the town.

I'm certain there was gossip about how Samuel came to be at Top Slack and why he walked with a limp – I heard one rumour that his leg was crushed by a falling stone and another that he fell from a ladder, neither of which we chose to refute. But there were few still living in the town who'd known him a soldier, fewer still who'd witnessed him fight, none who'd seen him desert the field.

Everyone said the war was over – that the King's army was in tatters – but still there was no peace and still there were soldiers on the streets of Middleholme (and in its beds and at its tables). Parliament had abolished feast days so there was no more dancing round the maypole, and no blood pudding at All Saints and no pilgrims at harvest time. Christmas became a day of fasting, not feasting – as though our lives were not bleak and colourless enough. Eli Braithwaite said that keeping feast days was a religion of works – that sinners mistakenly thought they might gain favour with God by their observance of such days when salvation was a gift of grace alone. Father said this teaching was scriptural and godly but Mother said it was foolish and miserable.

'Are we still divided?' I said, dismayed, as we made our way back up the cobbled causey path from church. 'Even though both my brothers are dead?' Samuel took my hand in his, swaying beside me with his uneven stride.

I looked up the fell and saw the Winstone Rocks leaning together like two cows on the brow of the hill. The sun was catching them so that they glinted silver. Suddenly, I heard Grace Fowler's voice, whispering to me, 'Meet me on the Hill of the Angels ...'

Grace

I do not know how much sorrow a human soul can bear. Ellen, my youngest sister – with cheeks as soft as peaches – died of a fever last month, a ragged rash creeping over her body like spilled dye. Mother, howling like a dog at the moon, has spoken nothing but gibberish ever since and becomes like a child who can scarcely dress or feed herself. Martha plucks at her skin until it bleeds and Margaret's face – once pink and round like the apples on our tree – is now pale as tallow. When I think that she is just ten years old I want to weep. She is the age I was when I first met Abigail Booth – when my life was all play and adventure and I heard the brush of angels' wings a dozen times a day.

Father has been gone four years now. I have given up all hope. I do not think that he is coming back. Skipton Castle fell and I have heard no news for these three years, so I can only assume that he is dead. There would be no home for him here now, were he to return. Middleholme is become a Puritan town. There is no beauty. Only sin.

*

I am so weary I want to lie down in the dirt. I am weary of being Jack. Weary of work and rough clothes and cold. Weary of wool – of drab, coarse, ugly cloth. Of hands that are red as rhubarb stems and cracked and raw and calloused as tree bark. And I am weary, too, of cruelty. It is said that Lady Hallam – following Sir James into Derbyshire – was taken for a whore and had her cheeks slashed and her nose slit as a sign of disgrace. Lady Hallam – with her gentle face and her coil of fair hair looping on her shoulders. I cannot bear it. I cannot bear all this violence and senseless suffering.

I do not think that God watches over us. I do not think angels guard our steps. I think the world is ugly and dark and that men's hearts are rotten as the stinking dung that swills through Middleholme's streets when the river bursts its banks.

Abigail

The cave was damp and smelled of bird droppings. A falcon was nesting there in the rocks and as I approached it swooped out through the crack between the stones, startling me with the speed of its flight. There were no angels in the cave and no Grace Fowler. Why had I thought she would be there? I had not seen her since the day my brother smashed the face of Jesus on the cave floor. Kneeling down I felt with my hands among the bracken and leaves and dried grasses that the wind had blown there and my fingers touched a sharp cold splinter of glass. When I stepped back out into the light a drop of scarlet blood was oozing from my fingertip.

*

That year – 1648, the year I was eighteen – we had the worst summer I can remember. For weeks it rained and our crop of oats turned black with mould. The ground around Top Slack was like a marsh and a huge oak tree slithered down the bank at Coldwater Clough, blocking the stream so that its water broke free and gushed down the field.

There was talk of war again in the streets of Middle-holme – rumours of battles, and armies and settlements. Some said the King had surrendered. Some said he was held captive on an island with no clothes. Richard Sunderland – whom I believed more than most – said the King's troops were mustering forces again and marching on Preston.

It was a Friday – market day – in late July when I went with my parcel of broadcloth, buckled on to Dandelion's back, to Thomas Sunderland's house. There was quite a crowd in the loom shed – weavers and croppers and dyers and spinners – all presenting their handiwork to Master Sunderland's sons and waiting to be paid. I saw Anne Sutcliffe, the tanner's wife – big with child – and Gabriel Cropshawe, who lost an arm at Marston Moor, and Anne Sowerby, whose raven-black hair had turned snow white since the war began.

Suddenly, a commotion broke out because a pigeon had flown in through the window and was flapping about our heads, clapping the air with its wings and throwing itself, panic-struck, against the window panes. Several people tried to grab at it or shoo it from the door but it only flapped more desperately until, tiring from the effort of trying to escape, the pigeon settled itself on a loom frame beside the window. Whereupon Noah Woodfield, the brewer's son – who is as tall as a tree – snatched the bird up in his bare hands and instantly wrung its neck, which caused a mighty clamour of cheering and laughter.

It was in the middle of this disturbance that I saw her. She was dressed as a boy – and a peasant boy at that – and

155

her barley corn hair was all hidden from sight but I knew her face, even from the side. And even after all this time. She was gazing sadly at the pigeon that lay lifeless and misshapen on the cropping table, alone in her lack of enjoyment at what had passed. At the sight of her, my heart leapt with joy. I wanted to call out her name but something stopped me. Instead, I watched as she handed a bundle of yarn to Richard Sunderland and held out her hand for payment. Then she stooped to lift a sack of wool and, heaving it on to her shoulder, walked towards the door. I hadn't delivered my kersey, but fearing that she might slip away and be lost to me again I dropped my parcel on the floor right where I was standing and elbowed my way through the crowds empty-handed. In the doorway Grace was speaking to Thomas Sunderland, her head bowed deferentially, her eyes lowered. I reached out and touched her shoulder and she turned and looked at me. Framing the shape of her name in my mouth, I was about to say it out loud when Master Sunderland spoke first.

'Abigail,' he said. 'This is Jack.' His eyes met mine, admonishing me with their stare.

'Jack?' I said, taking in her boy's appearance. Grace was looking directly at me, studying my face with her steely blue eyes. I noticed that her face was thin and pale and there were lines on her forehead like an old woman's face. I smiled at her but she did not smile back. Instinctively my eyes glanced at her hands – her hands, that had once been so white and soft and which were now as red as mine with their nails cracked and bleeding.

'Jack is one of my fastest yarn spinners,' Thomas Sunderland said and I nodded silently, struggling to take in all that had changed.

There were so many things I wanted to ask my friend and so I followed her outside. She walked quickly down the lane towards Market Bridge and I followed at her shoulder.

'Speak to me,' I said. 'Tell me all that has happened to you.'

'I cannot,' she said, hurrying away, lugging her sack of wool behind her.

'Your father?' I asked. 'Is he living?' Grace did not answer.

'I thought you had all fled with him?' I said. 'People said you were all gone north. Had I known you were still here, still in Middleholme . . .'

'I am not here,' Grace said. 'Jack Fowler is here. But not Grace.' She looked at me defiantly, her eyes full of fire. We had reached the bridge. The river, still in spate, was gushing underneath us so violently that I could barely hear her voice above its noise.

'Grace Fowler,' she said. 'Do you remember her? The Papist witch. The idol worshipper. The defiler of holy things, who your vile brother so despised?'

'My brother is dead,' I said quietly. She stared at me and her face softened a little.

'Both my brothers are dead,' I said.

'And my sister, also,' she said. 'And my father, too . . . for all I know.' Her eyes filled with tears. I wanted more than anything to take her in my arms and hold her but when

157

I stretched out my hand and caught her sleeve she pulled away from me as though we were enemies.

'Meet me at the Hill of the Angels,' I said suddenly but Grace shook her head.

'There are no angels,' she said coldly. 'It's only a trick of the light. That's why we only saw them when the sun was shining. Don't you know that? There are no angels and there is no hope. And in this new world you and I cannot be friends.'

She turned her back on me and ran, as fast as she was able with such a heavy load on her back, off down Southgate Street without looking back.

*

I went, with an aching heart, back to Thomas Sunderland's house to exchange my parcel of kersey. The crowds had all gone but the dead pigeon was still there – lying, twisted on the cropping table.

'That boy,' I said to Richard Sunderland. 'The spinner they call Jack? Where does he live?' The young master counted out my coins.

'In the cottages beside the West Bridge,' he said. 'The last one in the row as you go up towards Saltley.'

Grace

I hurry west along the banks of the Lumley, my wool sack heavy on my shoulders. It has begun to rain again and the path is slippery underfoot. The river, thundering towards Middleholme, rages past me, peaty and turbulent and whipped thick with foam. My feelings are turbulent, too, and my insides as churned and unsettled as the torrents of the stream. The unexpected meeting with Abigail and the kindness and softness in her face have unseated me. I had made myself believe she loathed and mistrusted me and now I see that it is not so. Did she really think me gone from Middleholme? And is it possible that she still dreams of angels? Still dares to hope?

I might have expected that news of William's death would make me glad. Did he not hate me and should I not then hate him in return? Is it not ignorant bullish folk like William Booth – men (boys, even) who think themselves possessed of The Truth – that have driven my father away? That have shackled my mother with fear so that she will not leave our cottage? That have forced me to conceal who I am and to work like a slave to stay alive? And yet, I find

159

I am saddened at his death. Appalled at the shock of it – that someone so young, so vibrant, so passionate should be robbed of life. Should be lifeless – senseless – as the pigeon mangled on the cropping table, which was one moment flapping and squawking above our heads and then in the next instant as dull and heavy as rock. I am sickened at the waste of life.

I am greatly saddened, too, that Oliver Booth is dead and I think now of his handsome smile and his gentle, calming voice, soothing Lady Hallam's fretting pony.

Suddenly, I hear the pounding of hooves and I step off the path on to the tussocky grass that edges the river bank. Three soldiers gallop by me towards Saltley. They are not Roundheads. Not Cromwell's men in their red coats. Their tunics are the colour of straw and their hats are broad-brimmed like mushroom tops. I have heard rumours that Royalists are coming again to Sir James's estate. I watch as the riders take the path behind our cottage and cross, at speed, into the parkland below the wood.

*

Reaching our cottage, I push open the door. My mother, seated in our only chair, calls out to me, 'Robert, is that you?'

'No, Mother,' I say, 'it's Jack.' The cat, who is now full grown and whom we call Shadow because of the way he follows us and wraps himself about our legs, trots towards me, his tail held high like a standard flag. I pick him up, hands a sling under his belly, and press my face into his soft fur. Mother is looking at me uncomprehendingly.

'I never had a Jack,' she says, her voice wavering with confusion.

I take off my hat and, smiling as cheerily as I can, I say, 'No, Mother. It's me, Grace!'

She stands up and, slow as sleepwalking, comes towards me, arms outstretched. As though seeing me for the first time, she runs her hand over my shorn scalp and says with horror, 'What's happened to your hair, Grace?' At her words I feel myself give way as a dam will burst when the river is in flood and the weight of water too great for it to bear, and I fall into her arms weeping.

*

That night I dream of the Winstone Rocks. The cave where once we stooped and crouched has become large as a cathedral and full of angels dancing. These angels are not specks of light on a wall, fragile and tiny as a child's hand. They are huge, luminous figures, tall as Noah Woodfield, with strong arms and thrashing wings and hair like rivers of fire. As I venture close to them their eyes seem to scald me and I feel the heat of their fiery breath.

*

I am awoken by screams and intense heat and smoke so dense that I can hardly see the mattress where I am sleeping. I hear my mother's voice, piercing through the hot night like an icy sword.

'Grace!' she is shouting. 'Help me!'

Abigail

I had strange dreams the night I saw Grace Fowler in Master Sunderland's weaving shed. I dreamt of twisted trees all stripped of their leaves and burning coals and a bell tolling. Of a moon the colour of blood and a man with no face and a thousand black crows falling from the sky. I dreamt, too, of Old Tristram with eyes bright as the stars, standing on Market Bridge holding a winnowing fork. I was an old woman with hands like a buzzard's claws. He was looking at me – as though his new-made eyes saw my very soul – and as he stared, he was pouring a sack of golden grain into the fast waters of the river.

I woke troubled and bathed in sweat and, creeping from my bed, pulled aside the curtain to the passageway, stepping through into the dark coolness of the workshop. Feeling my way past the silent handloom I walked to the window and looked out, down the hill towards Middleholme. There was a bright moon above the town. By its light I could see the river flashing in the valley bottom. Following the river west, my eyes took in its looping course and the dark, wooded hillside beyond with its shadowy contours. But then I saw a strange thing. In the sky above Saltley there was a deep orange glow. It was the sort of glow that often follows sunset, when the hills throb red and the heavens are all ablaze, and yet it was the dead of night when the sun had long since sunk below the moor.

I noticed a quickening of my breath and a tightening in my chest. Retracing my steps into the passageway I quietly unlatched the door and went outside. It was a warm night and the grass was moist with dew under my feet. I walked a little way to where the fell drops suddenly towards the wood below and sat down on a rock. The amber glow above the parkland seemed to be getting brighter. From my seat at the edge of the crag I could see further upstream from the town to the watersmeet where the River Lusk flows into the Lumley. And I could see the West Bridge, too. Suddenly, with a lurch of my stomach that felt as though I had fallen from a great height, I saw that there was another ball of orange light – smaller and much closer to the banks of the river. Saltley Hall was on fire and so were the cottages beside the West Bridge.

Immediately I ran inside and dressed myself as quickly and quietly as I could. Dandelion, dozing sleepily in the barn, one back foot resting on the tip of its hoof, looked surprised to see me and more surprised still when I led him, hastily, from his stall. Taking a length of rope and a blanket and a leather pail I climbed on to his back and dug my heels into his sides to urge him forwards. As I trotted past the front of Top Slack and on to the open moorland I heard Samuel at the doorway, calling out, 'Abigail? Where are you going?' but I didn't look back to reply.

We took the short route down the steep slope of the fell and into the trees beside Coldwater Dene. I was glad of the moon to light our path and of Dandelion's surefootedness on rough ground. At the bottom of the hill, we forded the stream, the pony plunging into the fast-flowing waters as I kicked his sides with my boots and clicked my tongue to encourage him. Scrambling on to the bank at the other side we galloped over the meadow towards the lane that crosses the West Bridge.

As we drew nearer to the cottages I could see that the whole row was on fire. Tongues of flame were spurting through the windows and leaping from the roofs and the night sky above was shimmering with smoke, coiling upwards. Dandelion was snorting and tossing his head in distress at the stench of burning. I slipped from his back and hitched his bridle to a post beside the bridge. Then, snatching up my pail and dipping it into the stream, I ran towards the fire. The moon, gleaming out from behind the flames, looked now like a disc of fire. As I looked up I could see great sooty flakes, like wounded crows, wafting in the uprush of heat and falling to the ground as slow as snowfall.

'Grace!' I shouted as I ran.

Grace

'Grace!' I hear my mother's voice, shrill with panic. The mattress where I sleep with my sisters is high on a loft platform under the eaves, at the top of a wooden staircase. I jump from my bed and stagger to the top of the ladder where my sister Margaret stands screaming. Down below is a vision of hell. Flames are billowing from the sacks of wool that stand under the window ledge and from the woollen hangings that are draped across the door. Beside the range, a bundle of logs is ablaze and fire is dancing across the woven mat that covers the floor by the hearth. In the middle of the room Mother, with Martha clutched on her hip, is beating at the flames with a brushwood broom. Suddenly a spout of flame shoots across the floor, consuming wisps of straw as though it were a monster gathering strength, and pounces at the leg of the chair, which catches fire in an instant. Mother turns and tries to stifle it with her broom but the heat is too intense and the bundle of brushwood itself bursts into flames. Mother drops the broom with a yelp. Martha is clinging to her, screaming and coughing in equal measure.

'Mother!' Margaret yells, standing rooted to the spot at the top of the steps.

As we watch, horrified, my mother's skirt catches fire, flames streaking up her back to her hair, which hangs loose down her back.

'Look out!' I cry and, pushing past my sister, I clatter down the ladder. There is a blanket rolled in the corner where Mother sleeps. I grab it and wrap it around my mother and my sister, slapping my hands against them to smother the flames. But now the table is alight and flames are leaping up the timbers around the window and doors, reaching ever nearer to the roof beams. I pull the blanket away and see, through the smoke, that my mother's clothes are blackened and torn. Martha has stopped coughing and screaming and hangs limp in my mother's arms. Instinctively, I push them both towards the door. We are only yards away but the heat is so intense and the flames so vigorous that it feels as if we will never reach the outside. The door itself is well ablaze now, standing between us and the night air like a wall of fire.

'Stay there!' I shout to my mother and leaving her for a moment I run to the back corner where the fire hasn't yet reached. Here there is an axe. I seize it and run towards the door. The axe is heavy and yet so gripped with terror am I that I scarcely feel its weight. As the door splits and breaks I hear Margaret behind me, calling my name.

'Come on!' I scream. Mother has now almost collapsed from coughing. I snatch Martha's lolling body from her as she staggers and falls to her knees.

'Get up!' I scream and I kick my mother roughly so that she gets to her feet again. Then I push her with all of my might towards the space that has parted in the burning doorway. Someone outside grabs her and hauls her free of the flames. I thrust Martha outside, too, and more arms drag her away from me. But now someone has hold of my arms and is pulling me out as well. Glancing behind me I can see Margaret, still stuck at the top of the ladder, flailing her arms like a scarecrow.

'My sister!' I shout and I wriggle free of their grasp and step back into the flames. People are dousing the fire with buckets of water now but, with the sudden draught from the broken-down door, air has rushed in and fanned the flames so that they leap ever higher. The foot of the ladder is now alight. Choking black smoke is filling my mouth. I pull off my shirt and tie it quickly round my face as a mask, in order to try and reach Margaret. I can no longer hear her voice above the crackle of the fire but I can still see her face, white above the flames, her mouth open wide in a scream.

'Jump!' I shout, reaching out my arms to her. 'Just JUMP!'

Abigail

On the riverbank in front of the line of cottages a bedraggled group of neighbours had assembled. Some were filling pails from the stream and hurling water at the houses in a rage of hissing and spitting. Some were huddled together in blankets watching with horror as the flames swept over walls and rooftops like hot floodwaters. A few people were standing round the lifeless body of a child, dousing her with cold water. Outside the door of the last cottage a woman, half naked and black with soot, was screaming and thrashing her arms as other women held her down.

'My daughters!' she wailed. 'My daughters! Let me go to my daughters!' As I drew nearer I realized that it was Grace Fowler's mother, though this howling madwoman bore little resemblance to the fine lady I remembered. There was no sign in the crowd of Grace.

Just at that moment the screaming woman broke free of her neighbours' grasp and plunged back into the burning cottage. I threw my pail of water helplessly after her and ran to the stream to fill it once again, wishing that I might somehow swallow the whole river and then spew it on to the flames in a great deluge. As I turned back I heard shouts above the fire's roar.

Grace

Margaret stands above me, her eyes wide with fear.

'Jump!' I shout again, my voice growing hoarse with shouting and with smoke. The fire has reached the roof now. It dances across the timbers of the eaves, swirling over the loft platform towards my sister, who stands frozen with terror. Suddenly, I see the straw and wool of the mattress catch fire in a ball of flame. A cloud of black smoke engulfs my sister so that I can no longer see her but I know, in that moment, that my last glimpse of Margaret's pale face with its staring eyes and silent screaming mouth will be with me all my days.

There is a crash behind me and I turn round, lurching for the door. Burning timbers are falling now from the roof, crashing to the floor in a splinter of sparks. Through the heat I see my mother staggering towards me, her hand over her mouth, her chest retching with the smoke. Then she stumbles and falls to the floor. A spark catches my breeches and the rough wool flares red. I slap at my legs with my hands, feeling my palms smart.

I can no longer speak, so choking is the smoke. My mother gropes towards me and I grab her hand. With the last of my strength I try to drag her towards the door. But as we cross the floor, a smouldering beam falls from overhead and my mother disappears into the burning rubble. I can no longer see where the door is, ringed as I am by ferocious flames. I am trapped. I am like Shadrach, Meshach and Abednego in the fiery furnace. The fire is so hot my clothes and skin feel as though they are melting on my bones. I feel myself fainting, sinking to the floor like candle wax. But just as I hit the ground I feel someone catch hold of me.

Abigail

The flames surging from the cottages were getting bigger and bigger so that our attempts to quench them with water were ever more futile. I stood, empty pail in hand, staring at the angry red furnace. The walls and window frames were starkly black against the flames now, like a burnt-out husk – a skull of a house, all its innards consumed.

In all the time since I arrived there had been no glimpse of my friend. Grace's mother hadn't returned from the flames and I heard a woman, standing beside me rocking a child in her arms, say, 'She's dead now, for sure – and all the bairns as well. There's none could stand that heat and live.'

But then, as if in defiance of the woman's words, I saw someone coming from the doorway, ringed with a halo of flames. His coat was on fire so that flames streamed from his shoulders like burning wings. It was a man, tall and strong, and in his arms was Grace Fowler. The man's clothes were so darkened with soot that, at first, I couldn't identify him. But as he laid Grace Fowler on the damp grass I caught a glimpse of his face, and a shock of hair, red as fire.

Grace

After I was carried half naked from the burning cottage there was little purpose in attempting, any longer, to conceal my identity. And so I became Grace Fowler again. Alone as I was now in the world, I was taken in by Thomas Sunderland to keep house for him and his three sons – to sew and make pies and puddings, as I had once seen my mother and Tabitha do, in the big stone house with the angel above the door.

This is where I am, in early February, when Master Robert arrives home from London. It is late afternoon and I am sitting in the parlour stitching a shirt in the fading light. There is thick snow on the ground outside. Earlier in the day, when running an errand to the draper's shop in Corn Street, I have seen the river frozen solid under Market Bridge.

Robert is very cold when he enters the house. He comes into the parlour, where a fire burns vigorously in the grate. I am seated close to it, because I cannot sew if my fingers grow too stiff with cold, though – heaven knows – the sight of flames still twists my innards into knots and the smell of burning causes fear to course through me like a mill race. I get up from my seat as Master Robert comes near but he gestures to the chair and says, 'Please, Grace, stay by the fire,' and so I sit down again and he sits himself on the settle opposite me. His coat, soaked through with riding into blizzards, is heavy and wet. He takes it off and spreads it on the hearth, where it steams gently in the heat.

Robert is the youngest of my master's sons and the one who treats me most gently. I feel his eyes watching me as my fingers work the needle backwards and forwards through the cloth. After a while he takes off his boots and stretches his toes towards the grate. Then he sighs and says, 'The King is dead.'

I stop stitching and keep very still, letting his words sink in, like a pebble thrown into a pond.

'I was in the crowd,' he says, 'when they took him to the scaffold.' I listen as Robert describes the soldiers who led the King, by the beat of a drum, from his palace, through St James's Park, to Whitehall.

'The River Thames was iced over like iron, Grace,' he says, 'and the wind was bitter cold. Colder even than Middleholme!'

He stares into the fire and frowns at the memory.

'The King wore a satin cap and, before he laid his head on the block, he tucked all his hair into it.'

'Did he speak?' I ask.

'Yes,' Robert says. 'But I couldn't hear what he said. Some said he swore his innocence and said the war was all Parliament's doing. Some said he spoke of liberty and duty.

I heard – in the tavern where I stayed the next night – that he said he was exchanging his earthly crown for a heavenly one.'

I picture King Charles in a crown that shines like the sun but his face is my father's face and his voice – low and warm and musical – is my father's voice.

'He stretched out his hands,' Robert says, 'and they killed him with one blow of the axe.' I gasp. Robert is scowling at the steaming coat.

'When the executioner held up the severed head,' he continues, 'I didn't hear a single cheer from the sea of people around me. Instead, there was a loud groan, as if the crowd, as one body, were mortally wounded.'

I look up and our eyes meet in the fire's glow.

'It is a terrible thing,' I say, folding my hands in my lap.

'What will God do to a people who cut off their king's head?' Robert asks, shaking his head. I am too choked with tears to answer him.

Abigail

The night we heard news of the King's execution there were violent gales in Middleholme. The sycamore tree in John Sowerby's garden crashed to the ground, making a hole in the roof of his house that let in the snow. Some folk said it was a sign that killing a king was an unnatural act and that the wrath of God had been unleashed. Father said it was the winds of change blowing, and that now that war was ended Cromwell would rule England in godly fairness and men would earn an honest living once again.

The day after the gales was a Sunday. It was also my birthday. I was eighteen years old. After church I went for a walk on the fell behind Top Slack. Samuel came with me and as we climbed up under the icy crags, I took his hand.

'The cave where I found you,' I said, 'there are angels there.'

'I know,' was all he said.

*

At the top of the hill a rabbit scuttled into a bank of snow and a buzzard circled hungrily. Approaching the Winstone Rocks I saw a trail of footprints – about as big as my own – heading in the direction we were walking, along the ridge towards the cave. The sky was heavy and grey, blank as Old Tristram's eyes. On the horizon above Saltley Park, bruise-coloured clouds were bulging with fresh snow. I stopped at the gash in the rock and listened. Someone was weeping inside the cave. Leaving Samuel and squeezing through the space in the stones I saw Grace Fowler kneeling on the cold floor. I knelt down beside her and, as I wrapped my arm around her shoulders, she leaned her weight against me and sobbed. At the sound of her crying I, too, found my eyes running with tears. They were tears of sorrow and of loss. Of waste and broken hopes and squandered youth. But they were tears of relief, also, that my friend was here, and rescued. Tears of gratitude and tenderness. And of love.

As I rocked Grace beside me I saw that in her hands she held a pullet's egg – white and smooth and perfectly unbroken. There were no shafts of sunlight spilling into the cave, no chinks of light bursting through the cracks. The sun was painted over with grey and the sky was thick as smoke. And yet, dancing on the wall above our heads were angels – fingers pointing and wings flickering. Three of them, and a fourth one – faint as a phantom – hovering behind.

Epilogue

Abigail Booth married Samuel the stonemason one year after the King's death. Their wedding was a plain and quiet affair and after it they continued to live with Abigail's parents, Silas and Elizabeth, at Top Slack on the hill above Middleholme.

Two years later – in the year of the eclipse – Grace Fowler married Robert Sunderland. By then Abigail was pregnant with her second child. The first child – a girl named Esther – had hair as black as a raven. By the time Esther was ten years old, and Grace herself had a son, Middleholme was weary of Cromwell's Commonwealth and there was talk of kings again.

It was in Lent of that year, 1660, that a servant answered a knock at the door of Thomas Sunderland's house. Grace and her husband and his father were eating fish at a table in the back parlour when the door opened and a man stepped in. The man was quite aged, with a lock of hair the colour of granite knotted behind his neck. He stooped a little as he walked and his clothes were faded and patched as though he were a tinker or a leech gatherer. When

Grace saw him she fell from her chair as though her bones had turned to water. Seeing her spread out on the floor her son ran to her in alarm, shaking her by the shoulders.

'Mama!' the little boy said. Grace Sunderland's husband helped her gently to her feet and as she walked towards the stranger, taking the boy by the hand, she said, 'Little Robert, this man is your grandfather.'

*

The Reverend Fowler celebrated Mass in Middleholme church in May, the day Charles II became king. It was sixteen years since he had last done so. The people of the town decked the church with apple blossom and the bells rang and rang and rang.

Later that day, at the house with the angel over the door, there was a feast. A goose was cooked and there were apple pies and raisin puddings and sweet wine that tasted of elderberries. Grace Sunderland, watching her father dandle her child on his knee, sat smiling in the window seat and looked northwards towards the hill. On the fell below the Winstone Rocks, bathed in afternoon sunlight, she could see people. Looking more closely she recognized a family. A girl running towards the crag and a boy behind her with hair the colour of rowan berries. A woman carrying a child on her hips and a man with flame-red hair following her with the faintest trace of a limp. They were making their way up the fell to the Hill of the Angels. And still the church bells rang and rang.

Acknowledgements

Most fiction is a weaving together of the real and the imagined. The idea of writing *Hill of the Angels* goes back to 2000 when I was Writer-in-Residence at Halifax Parish Church (now Halifax Minster) as part of the town's millennium celebrations. I was gripped by accounts of all that happened there during the civil wars of the 1640s and the intensity of political and religious beliefs that shaped the fabric of this period of British history. My story's themes – religious intolerance, the radicalization of young men, the violent destruction of sacred sites – have resonance now that they didn't have at the beginning of this century and the impact of civil war is all too evident in current situations across the globe.

Although Middleholme is a fictional place, it bears many similarities to Halifax in West Yorkshire. Some of the things that happen in my story – especially those concerning the destruction and preservation of the church – are based on historical events. Robert Fowler is modelled on Richard Marsh, the vicar of Halifax from 1638, who went into hiding when the town was occupied by Parliamentarian troops and returned at the Restoration in 1660. Old Tristram was a real beggar (there's a statue of him in Halifax Minster) but I invented his blindness and his role as a prophetic seer. Grace, Abigail and all the other characters are fictional creations.

I am indebted to the late Pauline Millward and to Alistair Ross for oral accounts and have drawn extensively on two books – *The English Civil War, at First Hand* by Tristram Hunt (Weidenfeld and Nicolson, 2002) and *Halifax* by John Hargreaves (Edinburgh University Press, 1999). The phrase 'Meet me on the Hill of the Angels' is inspired by the song 'Hill of the Angels' (Sticky Music, 2000) by my friend Steve Butler and used with his kind permission.

Special thanks to Carolyn Hopper, Laurette Thomas, Tim Mayfield and Tracey Messenger.